QUICK SILVER

SHERRYL D. HANCOCK

VULPINE
P R E S S

Published by Vulpine Press in the United Kingdom in 2020

ISBN 978-1-83919-602-7

Cover by Claire Wood

www.vulpine-press.com

Also in the *Wild Irish Silence* series:

♫ PROLOGUE ♫

Joe Sinclair was trying to find his girlfriend, Jordan Tate, and he wasn't having much luck. He'd called her house in Malibu—no answer. He'd tried her best friend BJ's house—no answer there. Finally he'd driven to the offices of Badlands Records, BJ's record label. Walking up to the receptionist, he smiled. The girl smiled back at the handsome man with the longish dirty-blond hair and light blue eyes. She thought he looked like a rock star, and if he wasn't one, he should be!

"Can I help you?" she asked hopefully.

"Yeah," Joe said, leaning on the counter. "I'm looking for BJ Sparks. Is he in the office today?"

"Uh..." the receptionist hedged—did the guy really think he could just walk up and ask for a superstar like BJ Sparks?

"Look," Joe said, noting the "this guy's nuts" look on her face. "My name's Joe Sinclair. If he's in, can you call him and let him know I'm here?"

"I'll check, sir," she said. Joe's name sounded familiar—maybe he was a rock star after all.

A few minutes later, Joe lounged in the lobby of the offices.

"Joe?" Tabitha Sparks queried as she walked out into the lobby.

"Tabitha, right?" Joe asked, remembering BJ's daughter.

"Yeah, hi." Tabitha smiled. "Dad's in a meeting, but come on back. You can wait in his office."

"Great, thanks." Joe stubbed out his cigarette and pushed off the wall he'd been leaning against.

"So, how are you?" Tabitha asked as they walked through Badlands' offices.

"I'm good," Joe said. "And you? When are you and Devlin going to give BJ some grandbabies?"

"Don't you start!" Tabitha exclaimed, rolling her eyes. "Dad's been hassling me for months already. I just got married, for God's sake!"

Joe chuckled. "Your dad isn't really a patient man."

"Tell me about it!" Tabitha said, laughing as she opened the doors to her father's office.

Tabitha Sparks was married to BJ Sparks' best friend, the lead guitarist of his band, Sparks. Devlin had known Tabitha since she was a baby. It had been quite a surprise when the two had fallen in love and gotten together. It had caused a lot of trouble during a tour featuring Sparks, Jordan, and two other big-name bands BJ represented on his label. Things had worked themselves out, but it had made for a lot of headlines for a while.

The rock-and-roll world definitely had its share of nice people. Unfortunately, it was still a bit too fast for his blood now.

"Do you want anything while you wait?" Tabitha asked.

"Nah," he said. "I'm fine. It's good seeing you again, Tabitha," he added, touching her on the arm. "You're as beautiful as ever."

"Such a charmer," she said, smiling and giving him a wink.

"That's me," he said with a grin.

Joe waited twenty minutes, standing and looking around Brenden's office. He was standing at the window when BJ walked in.

Brenden James Sparks was a self-made millionaire rock star and record producer. He'd come from nothing, and with an incredible drive, and an even more incredible voice to back it up, he'd made his mark in the music world. He was Irish, standing six foot three with long, dark auburn hair and incredible light blue-green eyes. His body was lean but well built. He had women swooning even after over two decades in the business. He was the best.

He was also Jordan's best friend. If anyone knew where she was, it would be BJ.

"Don't jump," Brenden said, grinning.

Joe laughed. "Not likely."

"What's goin' on, man?" Brenden asked, walking over to Joe and extending his hand.

Joe took his hand, grasping it and clasping his other hand over it. "Well, you know it ain't good, right?"

BJ made a face, then nodded. "You still got yer head. That's a good thing, right?"

Joe gave a short laugh and nodded back.

"Sit." BJ gestured to the comfortable leather chairs on the far side of his office.

Joe did, and BJ followed suit. The two men regarded each other.

"So, what happened?" BJ asked.

Joe took a deep drag on his cigarette and blew the smoke out in a long stream. "I can't keep up with her, man."

Brenden understood that. Jordan was a whirlwind, always on the move, always restless when she was in one place too long. She was quite exhausting as a best friend. Jordan and BJ had dated for years, so Brenden knew how much attention Jordan required constantly. She could be quite a handful.

"So, you're done?" BJ sounded neither surprised nor irritated by the idea.

Joe blew his breath out, nodding.

"And you're here to tell her, right?"

"I need to try and talk to her," Joe said, taking another long drag.

"That's not always an easy thing to manage with Jordan," BJ pointed out.

"I know," Joe said. "But there are things she's never going to get from me, and I know she's going to try to tell me she doesn't want them."

"Like?"

"Like kids," Joe said, his face serious.

BJ pursed his lips. "That's something she's always wanted in her heart. She just never figured on finding someone she wanted to have them with, ya know?"

Joe rolled his eyes. "Well, she's already tried to tell me she didn't want them really."

"She's lying her ass off, man."

Joe nodded. "Thought she might be. Why else would she bring it up?"

"Exactly," Brenden said. "And you don't want any more kids?"

"I've got two I never see now."

"Good point."

"I just don't see this thing going much farther with us, ya know?" Joe said, seeking some kind of validation from Brenden. If Brenden could understand it, maybe he could get Jordan to understand it too.

"Well, it isn't like you haven't given it a shot, right?"

Joe said nothing, knowing that it wasn't going to be easy talking to Jordan, no matter what he did.

"Have you seen her?" Joe asked.

Brenden nodded. "She's at my house."

Joe's lips twitched. He knew that if Jordan was hiding out at Brenden's it meant she was really upset. There wasn't going to be an easy fix—he had to talk to her.

"I need to see her, man."

"I know," BJ said, moving to stand. "You driving then?"

"Yeah."

A half hour later, Joe walked into BJ Sparks' mansion.

"Make yourself a drink." Brenden pointed toward the bar in the study. Brenden knew Joe needed it; he wasn't there to have an easy conversation with Jordan.

"Thanks," Joe said.

He was standing in the study, taking yet another shot, when Allexxiss, Brenden's movie star wife, walked in.

"Hi," she said hesitantly.

Joe had never formally met Allexxiss Ramsey. She was extremely beautiful, with golden-blond hair and rich blue eyes.

"Hi," he said. "I'm Joe Sinclair. We've never actually met."

Allexxiss nodded in recognition of his name. "Ah, yes," she said, walking over to him and extending her hand. "You're here to see Jordan, I take it?"

"Yeah," Joe said, not looking pleased.

"And I assume Bren is looking for her at this point?" Allexxiss smiled fondly as she said her husband's name.

"Yes, I've got him hunting her down," Joe said with a grimace.

Allexxiss laughed softly. "He has to do that a lot with Jordan," she said, smiling. She canted her head at the shot glass in Joe's hand. "And I'm guessing the conversation you're going to have with her isn't going to be pleasant?"

Joe looked unhappy. Allexxiss put her hand on Joe's, looking up into his eyes.

"He'd never let her fall too far, Joe," she said softly.

Joe looked back into Allexxiss' eyes for a long moment, then nodded, closing his eyes. It was what he needed to hear at that point. He needed to know that BJ wouldn't let Jordan hurt herself or get heavily into drugs again because of this breakup. He needed to know he wasn't ruining her life by taking his back.

"Thank you," he said, quietly but sincerely.

Allexxiss smiled. The door to the study opened, and Jordan stood there. Allexxiss glanced at her, then back at Joe. She left the room silently, closing the door behind her. Jordan stared at Joe, not moving forward. Her look was wary. She looked beautiful, as she always did, her long dark hair framing her face. Even in jeans and a white T-shirt she looked beautiful.

After a long minute, she walked toward him. He stood on the other side of the bar. Without a word she took the bottle of tequila from his hand, pouring herself a shot and drinking it. She wouldn't look at him. She stared down at the bar.

"You're here to break up, right?" she said tonelessly.

Joe winced at the direct way she got right to it. It wasn't how he'd wanted to start the conversation, but what could he do? Lie? He nodded slowly.

"I think it's better for both of us in the long run," he said softly.

She looked at him then, gold eyes blazing. "Then why bother coming, Joe?"

He looked back at her, his eyes telling her he knew she was getting mad already. She lowered her gaze again, mad at herself for letting him affect her this way.

"I came to talk," he said. "I don't want to fight with you, Jordan."

She nodded, knowing it was part of the reason he was breaking up with her. They fought too much. He didn't like to fight, not with his girlfriend.

He walked around the bar and took her hand, pulling her over to the couch and sitting down with her. He held her hand in his as he stared down at her face. She wouldn't meet his eyes.

"Jordan," he began. "I love you, okay? I do, but I can't keep up with you anymore. And it's becoming more and more obvious to me that we want totally different things in life."

"Like kids," she put in quietly.

"Like kids, yes," he said. "Jordan, you're right to want kids. You have every right to want them, to have them, and to be with a man who wants that with you. I'm not that man."

She looked at him. "But I can live without that, Joe," she said, her voice a soft plea.

"You shouldn't have to," Joe said. "That's the thing. You should have everything you want in life, not be tied to what you're stuck with because you met a man who's a lot older than you."

"But I love you." Her eyes searched his.

"I know you do, Jordan," he said, his expression reflecting the sadness he was feeling. "But it doesn't mean that I'm the only man you'll ever love. I came along at a time in your life when you needed someone to love you for you. I did that, and you saw how it felt to be wanted for yourself. But the fact is, we're so alike in a lot of ways, and totally different in others."

"Different how?"

"Well, I like my life stable. I like knowing where I'm going to be from one week to the next. You don't—you love being different places constantly. I thought I could adjust to that, but I can't, babe, I just can't."

She took a deep breath and expelled it slowly. She wanted to beg him not to do this. She wanted to tell him she'd do anything to keep him with her, but she wouldn't do it. Brenden had already drilled her on not giving Joe a guilt trip. He'd told her that Joe was a good man, that he had a right to be happy in this relationship too, and if he wasn't, it wasn't her right to keep him in it at all costs. Basically, BJ had told her not to be selfish. That if she really loved Joe, she'd want him to be happy. It pissed her off no end, but BJ was once again right.

"Jordan," he said, taking her hands in his. "I tried, babe, I really did. I tried living in your world, and being what you needed me to be, but I need some stability in my life. And by the very nature of what you do, you're far from a stable influence." He grinned on the last point, his light blue eyes twinkling.

Jordan smiled back sadly. He was right about that. She was far from the grounded homebody he'd been used to for fifteen years.

She looked at him, her gold eyes searching his.

"Tell me the truth," she said softly. "Are you getting back together with Randy?"

Joe said nothing for a moment. He knew it would hurt her to hear that he was, but he also knew that he couldn't lie to her now. Finally, he nodded slowly, his look pained.

Jordan nodded too, blinking back tears. She looked away, trying to regain her composure. She'd always known that she'd lose Joe to his ex-wife. Randy was and had always been the true love of his life.

She took another slow, deep breath and let it out in a sigh.

"I guess," she said hesitantly, "it's better that you're going back to what you've always known than leaving me for some slut that caught your eye, right?"

Joe stared down at her, not sure what to make of her comment. Then he saw her smile. He reached out and hugged her to him. She leaned against him and cried, allowing herself that moment of weakness with him.

"I'm not going to say I won't miss you," she said, her face still buried against his chest. "But I know that Randy's really been good to the two of us. So if you're back together now, it's for the best."

Joe said nothing, choked with emotion. Randy had been right—it was much easier to talk about breaking up with someone like Jordan than it was to do. He couldn't believe how well she was taking it either. He wondered if he owed Brenden a debt of thanks for that.

After a few minutes, Jordan sat back and brushed her tears away with the back of her hand.

"Are you going back to the department?"

"Actually, I think I'm still going to go with the idea of the bodyguard work," he said. He'd discussed the idea with her a number of times.

"So maybe if I need you some time, I can get you to guard me?" she asked hopefully.

"Free of charge." He winked at her.

She smiled sadly, then grimaced. "I don't think Mackie will guard me again, no matter how much I pay him."

"God, what did you do?" he asked, grinning.

She rolled her eyes. "I was a bitch—what else?"

"He's used to that, honey. Remember, he's married to Cassie."

"Oh! I'm telling her you said that!" she said, laughing.

Joe laughed too. "Great, I've already lost my partner."

"Oops," she said, widening her eyes innocently.

He narrowed his eyes at her but said nothing. Then his face grew serious. He reached out and touched her cheek.

"I need to know that you're okay, Jordan," he said sincerely.

She sniffled loudly. "Well, okay isn't exactly how I am right now," she said, putting her hand over his. "But I'll be okay eventually."

"Just promise me that if things get bad, you'll call me... okay?"

"I can't promise that," she said, shaking her head.

Joe winced. He knew he was asking too much. "Okay, how about promise me you'll call BJ, if nothing else."

"That I can promise."

Joe pulled her to him again and hugged her. He felt like shit. He knew he was doing the right thing, but it still hurt to hurt her. It was the right thing—it just wasn't something that could be made perfect right now. He prayed that, in the future, Jordan would find love again and know that he'd been right about this.

♪ ONE ♪

Dylan Silver lay in bed on his stomach. He had a pillow tucked under his chin, and his silver-gray eyes stared into space. His wife of eighteen years, Marissa, surveyed him when she walked into the bedroom. He was still damned handsome, she had to admit that, with his jet-black hair worn just below his collar, curling at the ends. He was all lean muscle. The tattoo of the black panther resting across his shoulders encapsulated his personality.

The deep soulful eyes of the panther were his expressive side; he could open up the world with a phrase in a song. Dylan had the instincts of a big cat, moving smoothly from one thing to the next, but he also had the patience of a saint. He could sit and wait all day for something without one indication of temper. In fact, in the eighteen years they'd been married, she'd never seen Dylan's temper. She'd gotten a sense of it a few times in the early years, but in the last ten years, things had been so distant and blasé between them, she knew he didn't bother getting riled about her at all anymore.

Marissa, still pertly pretty at thirty-five, recognized one of what she considered Dylan's sulks. She rolled her eyes.

"Now what?" she couldn't help but exclaim in obvious exasperation.

His gray eyes shifted to her as he rolled to his side.

"What?" he asked, his English accent still clear even after so many years in the States.

"What's wrong now?" she asked, her tone still irritated.

The merest flicker of amusement went through his eyes, then he shook his head. "Nothing wrong," he said calmly.

"You're sulking," she snapped.

"I'm contemplating," he replied smoothly.

"Same bloody thing, Dylan!"

Dylan gazed back at her, the slightest smile twitching at his lips. "Actually, love, sulking would be indicative of mournful discord," he gently informed her. "While contemplation is merely the act of considering one's options carefully."

"Well, excuse the hell out of me," Marissa said. "Sorry I'm not a genius like you, professor."

Again the grin played at his lips, his gray eyes looking at her from a far-too-handsome well tanned face.

"I'm not a genius, love," he replied, his voice still as smooth as silk. "I was only the one-forty range."

"Fuck you!"

"Well said."

Marissa stared at him. It irritated her no end that he could remain so calm all the time. What the hell was wrong with the man? He was a rock star in his own right, having been a recording artist for well over fifteen years. His band, Project, so named for school project he'd been working on when he decided to put together a band, had been to the top of the charts a number of times. There had been years when the money had just rolled in. Marissa had happily spent to her heart's desire. She'd earned it; she'd been married to Dylan long before Project ever got off the ground.

Project had been a simple bar band in Chelsea, London, when she'd met him, and he wasn't even the lead singer, only the bassist! She'd been interested in the lead singer, but his bitchy girlfriend had warned her off. Dylan Elliott—his given name; he'd become Dylan Silver later—had been a looker even then, and they'd gotten on rather well, so they'd gotten together.

When she was seventeen and Dylan was nineteen, they decided to marry. Marissa was no fool; she knew she was grabbing onto a good thing. Dylan's songwriting abilities were what made him the head of the band. He was not only good at putting together great melodies, but his lyrics made the songs legendary. He had an imagination that was unsurpassed in the business. And when he put words to paper, they flowed. He phrased things to create an image, a picture of what the words meant, and it kept Project on top for a long, long time.

Dylan never let the money go to his head. He spent minimal amounts. He drove a nice car, a Jaguar XKR. They owned a reasonably sized mansion in Bel Air. It wasn't as big as Marissa would have liked, but Dylan was always practical. Since they had no children, he didn't see the point in having a house with twenty rooms. So their estate had only six bedrooms, but Marissa made sure they were luxurious and had the best of everything. Dylan shook his head at the expense but said nothing. It wasn't that he was frugal; he just couldn't abide wasting money on senseless things.

Marissa and Dylan were about as different as night and day. She was the screaming fireball with credit cards. He was the even-tempered, mild-mannered moneymaker. They'd struck a balance in their marriage that kept things on an even keel. Marissa accepted all his little quirks, and he continued to keep her in diamonds and furs, or at least paid the bills that she ran up to get those things for herself.

After staring at him crossly for a few minutes, she sat down on the bed, giving him a annoyed look.

"So what are you *contemplating*?" she asked with acerbity.

Dylan grinned, noting that she just couldn't let it go; it was definitely her way. "We got the new deal today," he said unenthusiastically.

"And?" Marissa asked hopefully. She knew he was referring to the renewal of Project's record contract with Badlands Records.

"And," he said with a mild shrug, "it sucks."

"Sucks?"

"Like gravity on the Titanic." His grin was still in place.

"So what are you going to do?" Marissa asked, her voice shrill.

"Do?"

"Yes," Marissa said, making a face. "Do, Dylan, what are you going to do? Are you going to tell them it's not acceptable?"

Dylan looked mildly amused again, which annoyed Marissa more. "Not acceptable..." he said, as if testing out the term.

"Dylan..." Marissa's tone had become dangerous.

"Mar, look," he said. "It's a fair deal for a band that's tapped. I just don't know that I want to put out mediocre rubbish for the masses anymore."

"Tapped?"

"Tapped out. Used up, strung out, ready for the dung heap."

Marissa gave him a sour look. He was always coming up with new ways of saying common things. It drove her nuts trying to keep up with him. Most of the time she ignored whatever he said—that way she didn't have to pretend to understand him.

"You're not tapped out," Marissa said. "You just need another hit, is all..."

Dylan laughed, nodding his head. "That would be my point, love."

"Then sue the bastard!"

"Sue?" Dylan repeated in disbelief. "You want me to sue BJ Sparks because he won't pay me outrageous amounts of money for music no one is listening to anymore?"

"Well, you have to do something!"

"And so I shall."

"Good," Marissa said, thinking she had won this round.

Needless to say, she was shocked when, the next day, he walked into their kitchen and informed her that he was now officially unemployed.

"You're what?" she asked. Her look indicated there was no way she believed what she'd just heard.

"Unemployed," he repeated. "A miscreant, a layabout, a degenerate, without gainful employment."

"Don't start with me, Dylan," she warned. "I'm not even close to being in the mood for your shit today."

"Charming as always," Dylan replied sweetly, reaching for the pitcher of orange juice and pouring himself a glass.

"I can't believe you fucking quit," Marissa said when he said no more on the matter.

"I didn't quit, love." He picked up the paper and scanned it. "I merely indicated to BJ Sparks that it was in his best interests and mine to quit while we were still both ahead."

"You're a bloody idiot!" Marissa screamed, jumping up from the table and storming out of the room.

Dylan continued to read the paper calmly, sipping at his orange juice, one bare foot on the chair next to him, his arm thrown casually over his knee. Marissa seethed and stormed in the other room, picking up things and throwing them across the room. It took her twenty minutes to reach a suitable level of calm to go back and talk to her husband.

"So what are you going to do?" Marissa asked, doing her best to rein in her temper.

He glanced up from the paper, his gray eyes silver in the sunlight. He frowned in thought, then shrugged. "I'm sure something will come to me in time."

Marissa stared at him open mouthed, unable to believe that he was letting go of a career that had brought them millions. Was he really crazy? She was sure he was; he had to be.

To further substantiate her thoughts, two days later she walked into the house and heard the usual beat of music coming from his study. Walking in, she saw him sitting at his desk, happily paying bills and singing along to the stereo. Music was Dylan's entire life. He could live without food, water, even sex, but don't ever put him in a room without access to music. He'd literally die; he was convinced of it.

"We have an accountant for that," Marissa told him dispar-
agingly as she gestured at the checks he was studiously writing
out to pay their bills.

He looked at her, continuing to move his head to the beat of
"Heart Go Faster" by the Davey Brothers and singing the words.

"Dylan!" she yelled, trying to make herself heard over the
music.

He promptly paused the CD, looking at her quizzically. "Yes?"

She stared back at him in exasperation, shook her head, and
walked away. She didn't catch the quick grin as he picked up the
remote and unpaused the CD.

Dylan wasn't quite the idiot his wife thought him to be. He
was fully aware of their finances, how much she spent, how often
she spent it, and where. He was also in full control of all of his
faculties. Just because he refused to engage in constant battles
with her about money, his career, or her impoverished state of
living, didn't mean he was crazy. In fact, he was sure that not engaging in such nonsense with her over the years had kept him far
more sane than most men in his industry.

Dylan Silver was far more level headed than his wife gave
him credit for. He was also not as naive or blind as she thought he
was either. He was fully aware that she'd been having various affairs for years. It was fine with him, considering he'd been doing
the same. The fact that he didn't find it necessary to be totally indiscreet about his affairs, like she was, didn't mean he didn't have
them. He also tended to be much more selective of who he slept
with, versus her willingness to jump any warm body that seemed
interested. He didn't feel that it made him less of a adulterer, but
he knew there was a level he wouldn't sink to, and "as long as it
has a pulse" level wasn't his style.

What Marissa didn't understand about her husband was el-
emental. She didn't understand either his morals or his work
ethic. In a business rife with people with no scruples whatsoever,
Dylan Silver had them in spades. He refused to take money or

15

credit that wasn't due him, and he refused to fall into the star-trip slant on life. "I'm a star, so you, my public, owe me something" wasn't something Dylan would even consider thinking. Whereas Marissa felt that the public owed *her* something for her husband's talent. Dylan merely shook his head at her attitude and proceeded to ignore it.

Everyone in the business knew—if you wanted action, call Dylan Silver; if you wanted attitude, call his wife. Marissa Silver gave great attitude.

***

Jordan Tate lay on her bed in her Malibu home. The windows were open to let in the ocean breeze, but she didn't notice. The house she owned was a multi-million-dollar dream. Glass windows faced the vast ocean and rocky hills surrounding its private location. Lush gardens and trees filled the terraced yard that housed a huge infinity pool and hot tub. It was the best money could buy, and she had it all. And she didn't care.

I feel empty, was all she could think. She knew she had no right to feel empty. She was on top; she was a best-selling artist. A rock star. Her second album had gone to number one and stayed there. Her last tour had sold out everywhere. She was rich beyond her wildest dreams. She had a beautiful home, a flat in London, three great cars, and a jet to take her anywhere she chose to go. And yet... she wasn't happy. The natural question would be why?

Two years ago she'd been perfectly happy in her existence. Brenden Sparks, her best friend, and owner of the label she made albums under, was behind her all the way. They were sometimes lovers, most of the time friends. She'd lived everywhere. Jordan had grown up in Europe; her father was an ambassador for the US. His connections had gotten her the first audition for an agent. That agent had gotten her a record deal. BJ Sparks and Badlands

Records had been the deal. Her first album had done well—BJ Sparks had made her a star. She was wanted by millions, praised, adored, and sought after.

Then she met Joe Sinclair. She'd gone to a house party in London before her European tour. The owner of the house was one Joseph Michael Sinclair IV. Before she even met Joe she had heard various rumors about him. She'd heard he was a drug dealer, a murderer who'd killed his own parents to inherit their vast estate, and she'd also heard he was a cop from the States. The last had proven to be true.

Joe was a police captain in San Diego, California. He'd come home to England when his wife had decided to divorce him. He'd brought his two children back to his childhood home to hide out for a while. The party hadn't been Joe's idea—it had started out as inviting a few friends back to the house and had grown from there.

Jordan had found Joe Sinclair hiding out, more or less, on a back veranda of the house, watching his kids and other children play in the rare fall sunshine. Joe had a casual power that emanated from him. He was handsome, with shoulder-length dirty-blond hair, and the most beautiful light blue eyes she'd ever seen. On top of that he was intelligent. They ended up talking for literally hours that day and into the evening. In the wee hours of the morning, they'd ended up making love. It had been fantastic. They'd spent the next two weeks together before she left for her European tour.

During that time, Joe had told her about the situation with his wife, Randy. Randy and he had been married for fifteen years; she was the love of his life. But somewhere, somehow, things had changed between them. He didn't understand it, but he was willing to let things go the way they were meant to. Randy had been the one to file for divorce. She didn't want him anymore, and she was letting him go. Jordan did her best to help Joe make sense of it, but in the end she wanted him for herself.

Joe was the kind of man women dreamed of: handsome, gallant, sexy, smart, generous, and very romantic. One night when she was on her tour, she was in Paris and he was still in London, readying to go back to the States. They talked on the phone for three hours. She missed him terribly by that time, having grown quite used to falling asleep in his arms at night. She knew she wasn't going to be that close to him again for months, since he was headed back to America and her European tour was another month and a half. In the end, he'd surprised her by showing up at her hotel in Paris with flowers and a ticket for her to fly with him back to the States to attend his cousin's wedding in Vegas. She'd been overwhelmed by his thoughtfulness. He was the perfect man. At least she'd thought so.

They'd managed to stay together for a year and a half. The problem was that Joe was a cop in San Diego, with two kids and a whole extended family of people that counted on him. Jordan was a free spirt with tours to go on and places to be. They had a difficult time making their two lives work. In the end she'd bought him a plane, so he could fly to see her whenever he got the chance. But even that didn't work. He still had to be free enough to do that.

There were other considerations too. Jordan was only thirty-six; she'd never been married or had children. It was something she'd never really thought about. Being in love with Joe had changed that. She wanted everything with him. She wanted to share an entire life with him. The problem was, Joe was fifty and considered himself past that stage in life. He had two children with Randy, and he'd already done the marriage thing for fifteen years. He wasn't ready to get married again. At least not to her.

When they'd broken up, Joe had admitted that he was getting back together with Randy. That he needed the stability that life with Randy gave him. Jordan did her very best to understand, but it wasn't easy. She loved him, and he said he loved her, but that he couldn't be with her. What did that mean? She never really understood it, but that didn't keep the breakup from happening. So did it really matter that she didn't understand? Apparently not.

After the breakup, she'd gone about dating anyone who caught her fancy. She slept with them and moved on—they meant nothing. No one meant anything anymore. The only man she confided in was BJ. Brenden was the one man she turned to whenever she was out of patience for mediocre men. Brenden represented sexuality, masculinity, and power all in one extremely handsome package. They'd had an on-again, off-again romance for a few years after he'd made her a star. And Jordan knew that had he been single, she'd be his girl again now.

But Brenden wasn't single anymore. The love of his life from years past had come back. Allexxiss, known worldwide by her maiden name, "Ramsey," was a movie star. She was ethereal, beautiful, and unsurpassed at the box office for talent. With Brenden's music on the soundtrack, profits on her last movie, her first production, had gone through the roof. Everything Brenden had ever touched had turned to gold. Ramsey had the same gift, and together they were an unbeatable couple. Brenden was rock's baddest bad boy, but Allexxiss had tamed him. Everyone was astounded, everyone except the people that knew Brenden best. His good friends knew he'd never stopped loving Allexxiss from years before when she'd given birth to their daughter, Tabitha. Circumstances had kept Allexxiss and Brenden apart—nothing would separate them again.

Jordan understood why Brenden wasn't available to lean on now. But understanding didn't always make things easy. Jordan had made a point of staying away from Brenden, knowing that seeing him would make her ache for what she was missing. She also knew herself well enough to know she wouldn't be able to resist testing Brenden's dedication to his wife and that would probably end up hurting them both more. So she stayed away.

That worked, so long as BJ stayed away too. His having a key to her house didn't make that as easy as it seemed it should be.

"So, what happened?" Brenden asked, leaning against the doorjamb of her bedroom.

Jordan grimaced, knowing that he'd probably been standing there for a while. So he could see the disaster the room was in, her latest self-indulgent, destructive, furious, pointless rage. He could also see that she was a mess again.

"Nothing happened," Jordan said.

"Teddy just quit?" Brenden asked, stepping carefully over the broken glass on the floor and moving toward the bed.

"Teddy got a stick up his ass and wouldn't pull it out," Jordan sighed.

Teddy Harenden, the bassist for Jordan's backing band, had quit the day before. There'd been a raging fight between Jordan and Teddy. She'd flat-out told him to take his "no-talent, limp-dick self" out of her studio and not bother to come back. Teddy had slammed out of the studio and left the offices. He'd called BJ that morning to say he couldn't handle Jordan's temper tantrums anymore and that he was quitting. Brenden hadn't bothered to tell him that Jordan had final say on who her backing band was, so it wasn't necessary for him to quit—Jordan had already fired him.

Brenden had also had a full report of what had actually happened in the studio. He also knew that besides her heart not being in anything she was currently doing, Jordan was stone-cold out of inspiration for songs. She needed help. Brenden had already lined up help; now he just had to get her to sign off on it.

"Okay, so Teddy's out," Brenden said, sitting down on the bed. He reached out and smoothed her hair back from her face, his light blue-green eyes searching her face.

Jordan looked up at him when he said nothing else. Her gold eyes were dark and almost brown. It told Brenden a lot about how she was feeling. The more unhappy she was, the duller her eyes became. It was like watching her fade away.

"So, when am I going to get the lecture?" she asked tiredly.

Brenden smirked, knowing she was trying to get it over with quickly. "No lecture, love." He touched her cheek gently. "Except that you need to get out of this rut. It's going to kill you if you don't."

"You're one to talk, Sparks," Jordan snapped.

Brenden had been given to depression over the years, sometimes so severe he was hospitalized and put on suicide watch. Oddly enough, those depressions had all but disappeared when he'd gotten back together with Allexxiss. Another reason Allexxiss was worthy of holding on to Brenden.

"Don't get bitchy with me," Brenden warned, his tone not the least bit threatening.

"I am a bitch. You already know that, Beege."

"Yes," he said, his eyes sparkling mischievously. "But you need me right now, so you better be nice."

"Or what?'

"Let's just say I have a number of ways in mind to torture you if you don't shape up."

"Fuck you, Brenden. I'll shape up when I want to," Jordan said listlessly.

"Fucking me isn't an option, love," Brenden said, his thumb brushing her cheek.

"No?" she asked, sitting up. She was naked.

Brenden narrowed his eyes at her. "Evil, evil bitch." He shook his head, then poked her in the ribs with his index finger. "And you're losing too damned much weight, babe."

"I'm not trying, Beege," Jordan said.

"I know that." He picked up her bathrobe and handed it to her.

A half hour later he had her out of bed and out on her terrace drinking coffee.

"I have a partial solution," Brenden said, leaning back and stretching his long legs out in front of him.

"To?" Jordan asked.

Brenden grinned. "To your 'I have no bassist for my backing band' problem, love," he replied. "And maybe your creative block as well."

"You're buying me a dildo?" Jordan asked blithely.

"Oh, you are so funny," Brenden said, sounding like he thought she was anything but. "You don't need an actual dildo, love. You have all the men in the world to use as dildos."

Jordan raised an eyebrow. "Don't tell me you're offended."

"I am, as a matter of fact," Brenden said seriously. "You're better than that, Jordan."

"Yeah." Jordan curled her lips in disgust. "Aren't I though?"

Brenden narrowed his eyes at her. He didn't like this side of her at all. He much preferred his ever confident, brilliant friend. It annoyed him no end that he couldn't do anything about her current self-esteem issue. Before he would have happily reminded her what a beautiful, sensual and desirable woman she was. He would have reminded her with his time, his body, and his money, taking her everywhere, buying her anything, and making love to her anywhere the mood took them. But he couldn't do that anymore. It dragged at him that he couldn't help her the way she needed; he could only hope that she'd snap out of it.

"So, what's your solution?" Jordan asked.

"I have someone I want you to check out for the spot."

"Who?" Jordan asked curiously.

"Dylan Silver."

"Dylan Silver?" Jordan repeated. "Friend of yours?"

Brenden canted his head at her. "Now, I would think you'd know his name, since you listen to his music a lot."

"I do?" Jordan asked, looking perplexed.

"Project?"

"He's in Project?"

"He is Project, or was," Brenden said, making a face on the last part.

He wasn't pleased about Project not renewing their contract, but he couldn't help but respect Dylan's honesty about feeling the band was done making hits. He'd always liked Dylan Silver. He didn't understand the man, but he liked him. Dylan was the kind of person Brenden found very complex and impossible to figure out. While Dylan had all the money he needed, he didn't spend it, he didn't run around, he didn't get wild. It made no sense to a man like Brenden Sparks, who lived to be wild.

"Was?" Jordan looked astonished.

"Yeah," Brenden said. "They didn't renew their contract."

"Yeah, but… they're going with someone else, right?"

"No." Brenden shook his head. "Dylan said he thinks the band is tapped out."

Jordan made a shocked sound in the back of her throat. "But they can't be… I love their music!"

Brenden smiled, shaking his head again. "Well, unfortunately, their sales have dropped off drastically in this new age of meaningless junk."

"You canned them?" Jordan asked accusingly.

"No," Brenden said. "Like I said, they didn't want to renew. What am I going to do? Make them?"

"Yes!"

Brenden laughed outright at that. "I don't think so, love. Besides, you need Dylan right now."

"So who was he?" Jordan asked.

"Well, he was the bassist," Brenden began, seeing her unimpressed look. "And he wrote everything they did."

"He wrote their stuff?" Jordan asked, seeming both impressed and excited now.

"Yep." Brenden nodded. "I'm surprised at you, Jordan. He's won I don't know how many Grammys for his songwriting, and you don't know who he is?"

"Bite me," Jordan snapped. "I pay attention to things like album of the year, not songwriters."

Brenden shook his head and clicked his tongue. "Your lack of dedication to your craft shocks me."

"Yeah, yeah," Jordan said with a roll of her eyes.

Jordan knew Brenden did everything pertaining to the creation of his award-winning music. He was a master at his craft. Jordan was a graduate of the Musicians Institute in Hollywood, the top performance school in the nation. She was a master of her craft too; she just didn't take it nearly as seriously as Brenden did.

"So, you think you want to meet him?" Brenden asked.

"Hell yeah," Jordan said. "If nothing else I want to meet the man that's written such incredible songs for years."

"Yeah, well, you're gonna be looking at making him your bassist too. But maybe you can also get him to help you work on your songs."

"That's not part of the deal?" Jordan asked. "That he helps me write?"

Brenden shrugged. "I can't force something like that, Jord—either he's willing to help you or he's not. Your style is a bit different from what he's written before."

Jordan bit her lip, her mind already working. Brenden grinned. A new challenge for Jordan, and maybe she'd forget about Joe for a little while...

***

Dylan Silver stood in the outdoor atrium of Badlands Records. He leaned against the wall, smoking a cigarette. He was the picture of relaxed confidence. People walked by, nodding to him, and he nodded back, smiling. His gray-silver eyes surveyed the plants in the atrium as he resettled himself against the wall. Reaching into his jacket pocket, he pulled out another cigarette, lit it, and took another long drag.

Jordan was already a half hour late. Dylan didn't even glance at his watch. Brenden passed by, noting that Dylan was still waiting. Walking out the doors to the atrium, Brenden approached the other man.

"She's not here yet?" Brenden asked.

Dylan shook his head and shrugged, looking wholly unconcerned.

Brenden blew his breath out. "Way to make an impression, Jordie," he muttered.

Dylan grinned. "Don't worry about it, man," he said mildly. "This is my interview, not hers."

Brenden canted his head to the side, wondering if that's what Dylan really thought. He didn't bother to correct him, but Jordan needed Dylan much more than Dylan needed her.

"Let me know if she doesn't get here soon," Brenden said.

"Will do."

Brenden walked away, wondering at Dylan's endless patience. The man could be a bloody saint. Brenden knew he'd have been climbing the walls by now, but Dylan didn't look even the slightest bit irritated. It was amazing.

When he got back to his office he called Jordan's cell phone. She answered sounding harried.

"Where the hell are you?"

"I'm on fucking Sunset!" Jordan snapped. "I swear to God, you'd think these people never heard of the whole green-light concept."

"You're over a half hour late," Brenden said, glancing at his watch.

"I know!" Jordan replied. "I'm trying, Beege, I am. Is he there already?"

"He's been here for getting on toward an hour, Jordan."

"Shit. Is he pissed?"

Brenden grinned. "I'm not sure Dylan Silver knows how to be pissed, Jord, but I'm betting you're going to be the one to teach him. Just hurry up."

"Okay, okay!" Jordan said, hanging up.

Twenty minutes later, Jordan hurried into the atrium to see a dark-haired man leaning unconcernedly against the far wall. He was smoking. She walked over to him, noting that he was indeed a good-looking man. His black hair was worn slightly long, but not overly so. He had a strong jawline and smooth tanned skin.

When he looked up, the sunlight in the atrium caught his eyes, making them look like liquid silver. They were framed with thick black lashes. She also noticed that he had at least five earrings in one ear, and another four in the other. The earrings were in contrast to the black dress slacks, blue-gray oxford, and black suede dress shoes.

"Hi," Jordan said, smiling. "You must be Dylan Silver." She extended her hand to him. "I'm so sorry I'm late."

Dylan smiled warmly, showing perfect white teeth against tanned skin. "Not to worry. I had nowhere else to be."

Jordan found herself biting her lip, which she did when she was nervous. "Can I at least take you to lunch for being so late?"

"You drive, I'll buy," Dylan said smoothly.

Jordan was surprised by that, but nodded. She turned and led the way back to the doors to the atrium. Dylan opened the door for her, holding it while she preceded him inside and through the lobby. Jordan wasn't sure what to make of him just yet. Did him not allowing her to buy lunch mean he was a chauvinist? He was letting her drive, though, so that didn't really jibe.

Jordan led the way to her black Mercedes SL 600 Roadster, her latest acquisition, a $140,000 car with all the trimmings. Dylan noticed that it was parked at a haphazard angle, indicating that she'd indeed rushed into the offices. As they got into the car, Dylan glanced over at her. She was a very beautiful woman, there was no question about that, with her long dark hair and her amazing gold eyes. She was dressed in soft black leather pants, with black high-heeled boots, and a gold silk shirt tucked in at her tiny waist. Her makeup enhanced her perfect gold-toned skin, high cheekbones, and beautiful eyes. It was no wonder she was one of the most desired women in the world right now.

"Mexican okay?" Jordan asked.

"Sounds good."

Jordan smiled, turning over the engine. Music blared out of the speakers immediately. She grimaced and reached to turn it down. Dylan's hand on hers stopped her. She looked over at him; he was listening intently to the music.

"Linkin Park?" he asked.

"Yeah..." Jordan said, rolling her eyes. He probably thought she had lousy taste in music.

"This is *Meteora*, right?" he asked, naming Linkin Park's most recent CD.

"Yeah."

"I like this one. I have it too," he said, grinning.

"Really?" Jordan asked, her shock obvious.

"Yeah..." he said, tilting his head to the side. "That surprises you?"

Jordan considered for a minute. "I guess it did, but I think you probably appreciate their lyrics, right?"

"True," Dylan said, "but their music is very original, and I like that too."

Jordan nodded, looking as though she had just learned something. "I just figured you stuck to more... eclectic stuff."

"Eclectic?" Dylan repeated, amused. "In terms of what?"

"You know, like indie rock, or obscure bands..." Her voice trailed off as she realized what she was about to say.

So did Dylan. "You mean obscure bands no one has ever heard of?"

Jordan grimaced. That was exactly what she'd meant, and she was afraid her attitude about musicians that professed to like such bands was showing as well.

"And why would you think that's what I like?" Dylan asked mildly.

Jordan knew she was caught. Finally, she sighed. "I've been listening to Project since I was at MI when I was twenty-two. One of my professors thought your band was the be-all and end-all of lyrically driven music."

"Twenty-two?" he asked with a smile. "Two or three years ago?"

"Try fourteen years ago," she said, laughing.

"Ah..." He nodded. "That would have been our first album, then. It sucked."

"It did not!" Jordan said, shocked that he'd say such a thing.

"We sounded like kids who were thrilled to finally have a record contract," Dylan said with a smile. "Which we were."

"How old were you then?" she asked, curious about him now.

"I was twenty-three."

"So you're thirty-seven now?"

Dylan nodded. "I'll be thirty-eight in about two months."

"And I'll be thirty-seven in three months."

Dylan smiled. "Just bloody kids."

"That's right," Jordan said, more seriously than she'd meant to.

Dylan noticed but said nothing. They were both silent for a while as Jordan drove toward the restaurant.

"So, you have heard my music," Dylan said. "Do you think I'll fit in with your band?"

"I think you'll intimidate them," Jordan said, grinning.

Dylan looked surprised. "Why?"

"You've been in the business forever," she said. "They're all kids new to the business."

"By industry standards, so are you, Ms. Tate," Dylan said with a smile. "But I'm the one currently without a contract, so that doesn't say much for me."

"Beege said you turned down your contract," Jordan said. "That doesn't mean you weren't offered one."

Dylan smiled indulgently. "I can only rape the good public for so long to make a buck."

"What do you mean?"

"I just couldn't do it anymore." He shrugged. "And putting out mediocre garbage isn't in me."

"Excuse me," she said, narrowing her eyes at him. "I bought your last CD and I love it, thank you very much."

Dylan inclined his head to her. "You and about ten other people, which I figure were probably my family in England."

Jordan gave him a sour look. "Bullshit, you have millions of fans."

Dylan nodded, looking wholly unconvinced.

Jordan looked back at him for a long moment. She didn't think he was fishing for compliments. He seemed fairly convinced that he was on the decline; his not signing the new record deal attested to that. She wasn't used to rock stars that didn't consider their music the best they could do. Dylan Silver didn't strike her as cocky in the slightest. That was good, because if she was going to get his help with writing songs, she didn't want him thinking he was the reason the songs were hits if they were. She still had to sing the song, and perform it—she made it a hit. It was the reason she usually wrote her own stuff; she didn't want anyone trying to take credit for her success. She'd had enough of that in the past. Her stepbrother and ex-manager consistently took credit for making her famous. If anyone had done that besides her, it was Brenden, and Jordan knew it.

They arrived at the restaurant. Jordan was, as usual, mobbed by people wanting autographs. Dylan stood by, waiting. Not many people knew who he was, since he was a background man.

"Sorry about that," she said, smiling at him.

Dylan shook his head. "Nothing to be sorry for."

They were shown to a table and spent the next two hours talking in general about music. By the time they were lingering over wine, Jordan had decided she definitely liked him. He had a very comfortable way of talking. She could tell that he was very intelligent, but he wasn't pushy about it. He reminded her of Joe in that respect. The thing she'd liked right away about Joe was his ability to talk on a higher level than most of the people she dealt with. Joe had never assumed she was too stupid to understand what he was saying; Dylan was the same way. They discussed the intricacies of the music business, and Jordan found his views and ideas very interesting.

"Oh crap…" Jordan said, glancing at her watch. "I've kept you here for over three hours, Dylan, I'm sorry…"

Dylan smiled brightly. "It was time well spent," he said, his English accent smooth. "I haven't had anyone to have a good conversation about music with in years."

Jordan smiled back. "I have to agree with you there. Most guys I go to lunch or dinner with either don't know thing one about the music business or they only want to talk about how I can get them launched."

"Gad…" Dylan made a face. "That must be annoying."

"Oh, it is," Jordan said. "I make plans to go out with someone, thinking they're interested in me, and the next thing I know it's a three-hour audition."

Dylan shook his head. "That's why I stay in the background."
"You shouldn't."

"No?" he asked, grinning. "Why not?"

"You're far more handsome than I would have realized. You hid too well, I think," Jordan said, feeling suddenly reckless.

His silver-gray eyes searched her face. "But I can't sing," he said simply.

Jordan looked back at him for few seconds, then started laughing. "Didn't think about it that way," she said, shaking her head.

Dylan smiled, glad that he'd made her laugh. She was doing her best to be upbeat, but he sensed an underlying sadness to her. He figured it had to do with the very public end to her relationship with Joe Sinclair. Dylan read all the industry rags, always keeping up with the world he worked in. Part of that world lent itself to the worst gossip mills. Jordan's relationship with Joe Sinclair had been well documented. He wondered if her feelings for Joe went much deeper than anyone really thought. He also knew it was none of his business, but he suspected it had everything to do with the writer's block she was currently experiencing.

Looking at her, with the sun shining on her face, her gold eyes sparkling as she laughed, Dylan felt words to a song forming. It was his way—he would let the words flow through, and he'd eventually have a song.

"Excuse me a sec," he said, reaching into his pocket and pulling out a small pad and a pen. He jotted down the words that had just floated through his head.

Jordan canted her head to the side, curious as to what he was writing. His eyes flicked up at her, and he turned the pad around so she could see.

She read the words—"Halo of light, golden goddess of night"—then looked up at him.

"What's that?"

"Lyrics," he said, his silver-gray eyes looking into hers. "The beginning, middle, or end of a song."

"It just came to you?"

"Yeah," he said. "Happens all the time."

"Seriously?" Jordan asked, her look awed.

"Yeah," Dylan replied, wondering why she was so surprised.

She shook her head. "You have no idea how hard it is for me to write songs."

"Right now?"

"Ever," she replied. "But now it's worse. Nothing is coming at all."

Dylan nodded, wondering how much he should say. As usual, his need to be honest won out.

"If you don't mind me saying so," he began, his tone softening, "you need to take your pain and use it."

Jordan wasn't sure if she should be irritated that he presumed to give her advice pertaining to her love life. How did he know?

Dylan sighed. "I'm sorry, I know it's probably very presumptuous of me, and my wife will probably kill me for basically trying to talk myself right out of a job, but you need to use your life experiences to write. You need to just let your feelings flow onto paper and into your music."

Jordan said nothing for a few moments. "That's how I've always written before," she said eventually. "But this time, I feel like it's too personal, you know?"

Dylan nodded. "Sometimes it helps you just to put it down. It's cathartic to write, even if you never use anything you put down."

Jordan knew he was right. "So your wife will kill you?" she asked after a few minutes.

Dylan laughed. "She's not sure where my next million is coming from. That upsets her."

Jordan stared back at him, not sure how to take his comment. His silver-gray eyes sparkled in amusement, and it had Jordan laughing again. He was definitely a different kind of man, and she definitely liked him.

On the way back to the studios, Dylan's cell phone rang.

"Excuse me," he said, politely, pulling his phone out of his pocket and rolling his eyes self-deprecatingly.

Jordan could only hear his side of the conversation for the most part, but it was definitely an insight into Dylan Silver.

"Hello?" Dylan answered. "Hey." He listened for a moment, his eyes rolling heavenward again. "No, I didn't get it yet," he said calmly, his silver-gray eyes staring out the window ahead. "Yes, I saw him, but he didn't exactly have the check with him." A note of amusement crept into his voice.

His amusement was obviously apparent to the caller as well, because Jordan heard a woman's voice screech as Dylan held the phone away from his ear. When the receiver was silent again, Dylan put the phone back to his ear. "I understand," he said, his face serene.

"So, you'd like me to check with Tabitha and see if the check is in, I take it?" Again the phone screeched; again Dylan held it away, and a slight grin crossed his features. Jordan watched in fascination, while trying to pay attention to the road as well.

"Is the bank account empty?" Dylan asked mildly when he put the phone back to his ear. "I see." He nodded. "So, she needs how much?" His eyes widened slightly. "She wants ten thousand for a consultation?" he asked, disbelief in his voice. "She better give good head for that," he said, his tone amused again. He was rewarded with a screech yet again; he held the phone away, glancing over at Jordan, who was doing her best not to laugh.

Silver light danced in his eyes as he continued to hold the phone at a safe distance. Jordan could see that nothing the caller, presumably his wife, had said had irritated him in the slightest, not even the screaming tantrum she was having.

When he put the phone back to his ear, Dylan was still the picture of serenity. "Frankly, love, I don't see the point in redecorating at this juncture," he put in, withstanding the screamed answer with calm silence. "Why don't we discuss it when I get home?" he offered amiably. Once again there was screaming.

Jesus, Jordan thought, *does this chick know how to talk?* It was apparent that Mrs. Silver was given to tantrums, and her husband's neutral reception of those tantrums only served to irritate her more.

When he finally hung up, Jordan looked over at him. Totally unruffled.

"Your wife?" she asked mildly.

"Oh yes," Dylan said, rolling his eyes again.

"She always scream like that?"

Dylan considered the question, then nodded. "Pretty much."

Jordan shook her head. "I couldn't handle someone screaming at me like that all the time. I'd snap."

Dylan shrugged. "No point in engaging her when she's like that," he said. "It only incites her further."

"Further?"

Dylan didn't answer, merely quirking his lips in a grin.

Jordan said nothing; it was none of her business. She couldn't fathom how Dylan Silver put up with a wife that yelled at him constantly. He took everything so calmly—it was surprising that he didn't react at all to whatever his wife said. Jordan knew she had heard words like "fucking bastard" screamed at him.

Later that afternoon, Jordan knew she had to satisfy her curiosity about Dylan and his wife, so she started doing some checking. She saw pictures of Marissa Silver, and read about the screaming fits she'd thrown in any number of restaurants. Jordan also saw pictures of Dylan standing by, his face a calm mask as his wife threw her tantrums. The stories also often listed how "Mr. Silver" always handsomely tipped the waiters, waitresses, and hosts that had dealt with his wife.

Dylan Silver was considered one of the nicest guys in the rock world. There were numerous quotes by women in music, movies, and TV saying that Dylan was the best man alive. One woman, an extremely famous star in her own right, had been quoted as saying, "Dylan Silver is a poet, the best poet." It was a strange quote, and when the interviewer had asked for clarification the blond actress had merely smiled, her bright blue eyes twinkling. It made Jordan wonder herself: what did that mean?

Dylan's wife, however, was considered the biggest bitch associated with the music industry. So why was he with her? When all these other women thought he was "just incredible," "a poet," "fantastic," and "a prince." It didn't jibe.

Jordan read that they'd been married for over eighteen years. He'd been living with that for all that time? Poor guy. And that's how Jordan started to think of Dylan, as the poor humble soul that had a shrew for a wife. He must love her, otherwise why would he stay with her?

***

The first time they got together to work on music, Dylan showed up in the studio wearing casual black cotton pants, a gray and black patterned shirt, and Birkenstock sandals. He was very much a laidback man. He handed her three sheets of paper.

"What's this?" she asked, glancing at the neatly typed sheets.

"Ideas," he told her with a grin.

Jordan read the ideas and loved them all. Dylan was definitely a master at songwriting. He had a gift. They spent two hours in the studio, but Dylan said it was too quiet. Jordan had noticed the way his foot bounced as they sat talking about ideas.

"What do you want to do?" she asked.

Dylan shrugged, glancing at his watch. "Grab some lunch, and go sit on the beach?"

"And work on songs?" Jordan asked cynically.

"You don't have to be in a studio to write a good song, Jordan." Dylan smiled.

"I always have been," she said sourly.

"Best song I ever wrote," he said, leaning back in his chair, "was written on the Tube in London, on the back of my ticket."

"Are you serious?"

"Yes."

"Which song?" she wanted to know.

"The Hidden."

"Holy shit! Are you serious?" she asked, recognizing the multi-million-dollar single from Project's second album.

Dylan nodded, his silver-gray eyes sparkling.

"Hell, let's get to the beach!" she exclaimed, laughing as she stood up.

Dylan stood as well, looking at her. She looked fantastic as usual. Even when she wasn't dressed up, she looked good. She had a very natural sensual beauty about her. He wondered idly if that translated itself in more intimate situations. He'd bet his Jaguar it did.

Dylan knew he wanted her, but he also knew he wasn't going to push anything with Jordan Tate. She was the woman currently paying his salary, for one thing. He was also fairly sure she was still reeling from the breakup with Joe Sinclair, and he wasn't about to push her for anything that would only be casual anyway. If she was interested in him, she'd make a move. Shyness wasn't one of Jordan Tate's personality traits. Patience was definitely one of Dylan's.

In the end, they spent the day out at the beach. Dylan threw out ideas for songs, and Jordan loved everything he came up with. At this point they were simply going over ideas. Dylan said that it was better to take down everything they could think of, then see what went together and where. Jordan was willing to take his advice, since he gave it without a hint of superiority. She also knew she was dealing with a Grammy-winning songwriter. Brenden had told her in no uncertain terms that she needed to get on the ball with her latest album; she'd already wasted almost three months of studio time for nothing. Even Jordan Tate couldn't cost Badlands Records money like that and not produce. Jordan was desperate, and Dylan Silver seemed to be the one to help her out.

"So, if we went for a theme," Jordan said, leaning back and letting the sun warm her face, "I don't want to go too dark."

"But dark is how you feel, isn't it?" Dylan dropped back onto the sand next to her, his eyes closed.

"Yeah, but I don't think it's something my fans really want to see."

"Your fans want to feel your life," Dylan said. "They want to feel what you're feeling."

"You think so?" she asked, glancing over at him.

"Look at No Doubt. Gwen Stefani writes from her heart—her breakup with her guitarist was all over their first few albums. It's where her head was at. And now she's married, and happy, likely bound for motherhood anytime now, and her music reflects it."

"Hmm…" Jordan sighed, closing her eyes. "I don't think that'll ever be me."

"What won't?" Dylan turned on his side to face her, propping his head up with an elbow.

Jordan frowned. "Married, and happy, or having a baby at some point." Her addition revealed her true concern.

"Jordan, you're only thirty-six."

"Only? Women usually have babies in their late twenties, Dylan, not late thirties, and that would mean I'd have to find someone really soon, wouldn't it?" she said wryly

"Not necessarily," Dylan said. "Women have babies all the time without men involved other than for donation."

"Eh, not my style," Jordan said, wrinkling her nose.

Dylan smiled at the face she made. "Well, I was just making a point."

"Well, I want a man to marry me, and then I'll have a baby. To hell with that single-mother crap."

"Very politically incorrect, Jordan," Dylan said, an easy grin on his lips.

"Yeah? Bite me," she said, laughing now. "I'm not raising some screaming brat by myself."

"Screaming brat…" Dylan echoed. "You've got the loving-mother terms down already, I see."

Jordan laughed, shoving at his shoulder and making him drop onto his back. It seemed totally natural to lean up over him as they continued to talk.

His cell phone rang.

"Excuse me," he said, pulling the phone out of his pocket. Jordan stayed where she was, interested in this conversation. Wondering if it would be the same as the last. She knew she was being rude, but she listened anyway. Right away, she could tell it wasn't his wife.

"Hello?" he said into the phone. A smile appeared on his lips. "Maggie, how are you?" he asked warmly. "Uh, no, I didn't... should I have?" he asked, his silver eyes looking up at Jordan for a second. Then he squeezed his eyes shut and grimaced. "God, you didn't... Tell me you didn't really say that," he said, a smile on his lips again. He shook his head. "Yes, but why did you have to put it quite that way?" he asked, not sounding upset at all. He laughed out loud. "Okay, you win, you're in the lead... Okay, I'll talk to you soon... Yeah, sure, just let me know when, okay? Great, bye, Maggie."

He hung up, putting his phone away.

Jordan wondered if she could get away with asking if that was indeed Maggie Turner, the woman quoted as calling him "a poet." Instead she decided to go back to their previous conversation.

"So what about you, Mr. Silver?" she asked, raising an eyebrow. "Do you have kids?"

"Nope." He shook his head, his eyes silver in the sunlight. "At least none that I've been informed about," he said with a grin.

"Oh, hold..." Jordan said, her eyes widening. "Are you saying it's possible?"

Dylan looked contemplative for a moment then shrugged. "Anything's possible."

Jordan narrowed her eyes at him, sensing he was evading the actual question. "You're thirty-seven and you've been married for eighteen years... so you were all of nineteen when you got married," she rattled off, surprising him. "So, are you saying that there's a chance of that since you've been married?"

Dylan looked back at her for a few seconds, then a smile spread across his face. "Are you asking me if I'm faithful?"

"Duh," Jordan said, rolling her eyes.

"No," Dylan said simply.

Jordan was surprised, and she was surprised that she was. She'd gotten it into her head that Dylan must love his wife to put up with the verbal abuse she seemed to hurl in his direction a lot. In loving her, it must mean that he never cheated on her, right? Wrong.

"I've surprised you again," Dylan surmised.

"Yes, you have."

"And you think I'm a cad now?"

"No," Jordan said, giving him a shocked look. "I think you're human."

An amused grin crossed his lips. "And that surprises you?"

"No!" she exclaimed, giving him a narrowed look. "Will you quit that?" Then she shrugged. "I just did some reading on you and your wife, and if you'll forgive my saying so, she seems like a real shrew. So I figure you must be some kind of saint for having put up with her for that long."

"I'm no saint," Dylan said softly.

Jordan suddenly felt like she was being drawn in by his eyes. She felt his hand on her back, sliding up to touch the back of her head. Their eyes stayed connected, and Jordan knew she was going to kiss him; there was no way she couldn't right now. Everything slowed down. She felt the slightest pressure of his hand on her head, and she responded. Leaning down, she put her lips to his. His fingers slid through her hair, pulling her closer as his lips began a slow, deliberate exploration of hers. Her hands were on his chest, steadying herself, but there was no steadying her nerves.

His lips were strong and sensual as they moved expertly over hers. There was no hesitation, but no rush. She felt his fingers caress the back of her neck gently, his lips sucking at hers just enough to incite excitement in her body. She couldn't believe this. He was making her want him with a simple kiss. It hadn't been that long since she'd had sex, Jesus! It wasn't a heated embrace, more of a slow burn… It was like he was wandering through her body lighting candles one by one.

By the time their lips parted, Jordan was trembling. It was as if her body knew something and wanted to explore what else there was with him. A thrill went through her as she realized she was practically lying on top of him. She could feel his desire for her, there was no mistaking it, and that excited her more.

"Dylan…" she began, her voice husky.

"Mmm… I know," he said, his voice deeper, and with such a sexy timbre to it that Jordan frankly didn't care if they made love right there on the sand.

"My house is just down the beach."

"Convenient."

"Necessary, right now," she said, giving him a meaningful look.

Dylan grinned. He rolled to his side, then stood, taking her hand and pulling her off the sand and up against him. She leaned in, enjoying the sensual thrill that went through her when his hands slid around her waist and his lips nuzzled her throat. Closing her eyes, she wrapped her arms around his neck. She was surprised when he lifted her off her feet, putting his arm under her knees to carry her back to his Jaguar that waited in the parking lot.

On the short drive to her house, Jordan closed her eyes and settled back in the comfortable leather seat, her hand in his. Even that excited her; his thumb brushed back and forth over hers, rubbing inward over the space between her thumb and index finger. She never would have imagined it, but that spot had a sensual feel to it, or maybe it was just him, or the situation, she wasn't sure.

At her house, he pulled the Jaguar smoothly to a stop. He got out and walked around to open her door for her, taking her hand to help her out. It was a very gentlemanly gesture. When he gently pulled her up out of the seat and into his arms, however, every nerve in her body started again. They kissed, and Jordan lost all track of her senses. His hands were like live wires, sending pleasurable sensations down every part of her body he touched. It took them twenty minutes to get inside the house.

Once inside, Dylan pulled away and looked around him, taking in her house. She did her best to show him around, but the minute they got to her bedroom she gave up playing hostess. Leaning against him, she pulled his head down to hers to kiss him again. His hands reached between them, cupping her face, his thumbs brushing the corners of her mouth. His kiss intensified, his tongue coming into play, making her feel weak.

Jordan could feel the rest of her body burning to be touched, but for once she wanted to let him have his way. Usually she'd insist that a man touch her where she wanted to be touched, but somehow she sensed that Dylan Silver did things his way in this arena. The idea of him being a meek man suddenly didn't seem to jibe with what she sensed in him. Something in her head told her that he was a master at this, and she was willing to let him show her everything he knew.

By the time he finally moved her toward the bed, Jordan was holding on to him, sure she couldn't stand anymore. His lips moved from her lips, down her neck, his teeth grazing her skin, making her gasp out loud with the heat that sent through her body. She realized suddenly that his hands hadn't even touched her bare skin yet; it made her anticipate this with more longing than she'd felt in a long, long time. When his lips continued their leisurely but sensual exploration of her neck, she couldn't hold back anymore.

"Dylan, please…" she begged, grasping at his shoulders, willing him to touch her.

In response to her plea, his lips moved back to hers, making her forget for a full five minutes what she'd begged him for. His lips kept her so exquisitely entranced she couldn't think. So much so, that when he did tug her shirt out of her jeans she didn't even notice—that was, until his hands finally slid up under the shirt and touched her bare back.

Her immediate reaction was to moan loudly against his lips; her next reaction was to press against him. Suddenly he didn't seem nearly as slim as he'd seemed to her before. Suddenly he was a solidly built man, and one she wanted desperately, right now.

His hands, much like his lips, which continued to excite her senses, took their time in caressing her skin, exploring it, molding it, smoothing over her body. Jordan was shaking within minutes. He had a sensual but strong way of touching. It wasn't in any way hesitant—it was like he'd been making love to her for years. Her body responded instantly to every movement. And he hadn't even touched her anywhere actually intimate yet, only her back.

Her body was on fire. There was no way she could handle this, but it felt so good, and he tasted so good. He tasted like a mixture of mint and the sweet tobacco of his Turkish cigarettes. The scent of him, a rich combination of the smoke that clung to him and the woodsy scent of his cologne, was heady suddenly. Everything combined to make her want him so much she couldn't believe it. Suddenly he was taller, broader, and stronger than she'd thought him to be. His manner, usually so mild and easy-going, was now masterful and completely in charge, and it excited her no end.

She finally regained her senses long enough to pull at his shirt, not bothering to stop at getting it out of his pants, but pulling it all the way off and tossing it aside. What greeted her shocked her. The chest she'd imagined to be skinny was far from it. He wasn't bulky, but lean like a swimmer. Every muscle in his chest and abdomen was well defined. Her hands slid up his chest, her eyes reflecting her awe at having uncovered something so un-expected.

Her eyes connected with his, and she could see the heat in them. They were a molten heated silver now, like mercury. He grinned at her look, knowing exactly what had her surprised—he'd heard it before. "Jesus, you have a body under those clothes!" had been what he'd heard most. His clothes, always worn loose, hid the strength his body housed. He didn't run and work out for the way it made him look, but for the endurance it gave him. En-durance Jordan was about to gain a great deal of respect for.

His lips covered hers again, and Jordan had no chance to make a comment about his hiding that incredible chest from her. He finally removed her shirt, sliding his hands reverently over her skin, his lips following as he took his time exploring her body. He pushed her gently down to sit on her bed and kneeled on the floor between her legs. His mouth, hands, and tongue made her put her hands to his head, wanting him so much.

When he had finished exploring her upper torso, breasts, and stomach, he pulled her up to stand in front of him. Slowly he unbuttoned her jeans, his silver eyes staring up into hers. Jordan found she couldn't look away from him. It was like she was hyp-notized by him, wanting to catch every look, every nuance of his movements. When she pulled her jeans off, he slid his hand back up her legs. She shivered uncontrollably. He gently sat her back down on the bed. His hands slid down her legs again and began caressing her, starting at her calves. His lips soon followed. It was an extremely sensual massage, and Jordan was in heaven. *This man is a god.*

When he finally made love to her, Jordan was sure she couldn't handle any more pleasure, but even his lovemaking took time. By the time she'd come no less than five times, and he'd fi-nally allowed himself a release that had her coming a sixth time, stronger than the previous five times combined, it had been six hours since they'd begun making love. Jordan couldn't believe it. It was dark outside.

"Oh... my... God..." she said, still panting, as she glanced at the clock.

Dylan lay on his back, breathing heavily but not nearly as heavily as her. He grinned.

"What?" he asked, sounding very English.

"Six hours?"

Dylan only grinned again, reaching out to touch her cheek.

"What kind of god are you?" she asked, still a bit breathless.

He chuckled warmly, turning onto his side to face her. His hand slid from her hip to her torso, slowly, sensually, making her shiver.

"I'm no god," he said, looking into her eyes. "I love everything about women. I love the way they look, the way they smell, the way they feel." Leaning in, he kissed her lips, sending all kinds of thrills through her again. "I love the way they taste," he said pointedly. "I also love the way they sound," he continued, his lips on her neck, "when they're pleasured, and I love nothing more than finding what excites them."

Jordan was already feeling her body tingle again. "Oh God..." she murmured. "You *are* a poet..." That's when it clicked.

She pulled back. "That's what she meant..." Dylan looked back at her, perplexed. "Maggie Turner, that's what she meant when she told *People* that you are a poet. She meant this, didn't she?" She gestured to their bodies.

Dylan shook his head. "I have no idea what she meant exactly."

"But you did sleep with her, didn't you?"

Dylan rolled his eyes, a guilty grin crossing his lips.

"Oh my God, you slept with all of them, didn't you?" She should have guessed that was the reason for the glowing terms. Of course, she'd had no clue that he was quite the lover that he was until a few hours ago.

"Jesus, you definitely don't slum it where women are concerned, do you?" she said, remembering the names of all the women who'd had wonderful things to say about Dylan Silver.

His lips claimed hers again for a few long moments, then he pulled back. "I'm very particular about who I sleep with, and I have extremely good taste in women."

Jordan smiled. It was a very smooth way to get around the amount of famous women he'd slept with.

"Wait a minute... You slept with Billy Montague-Kristiani?" she asked, remembering that Billy had said that Dylan Silver was a god amongst men.

"Before she was ever Mrs. Kristiani, thank you very much," Dylan said, grinning.

Jordan shook her head. "You ever meet Skyler Kristiani?" she asked out of curiosity.

"Ah, no," Dylan said, putting a finger to the bridge of his nose. "He's a nice guy."

"Yeah, with a very jealous streak."

"True," Jordan agreed. "Although I haven't heard of him killing anyone yet."

"Yet," Dylan echoed with a chuckle.

They were both quiet for a bit, lying together companionably. His hand was on her stomach, his fingers moving over her skin with feather-light touches. He leaned down and kissed her lips, grasping her waist and pulling her to him as he deepened the kiss again.

"Mmm..." she murmured. "You'll get me going again, and it'll be at least another six hours..."

"And that would be totally acceptable," he said with a grin. "But I'm starving."

Jordan laughed. "I guess that would be normal, considering we didn't eat much for lunch..."

"I feel like cooking," he said, moving to sit up.

"Well, there's a kitchen full of groceries downstai—Oh my God!" she exclaimed as he sat with his back to her.

"What?"

She sat up, sliding her hands over the black panther tattoo over his shoulders. "This is incredible," she said, noting the exquisite detail and coloring of the tattoo.

"Oh." He nodded. "I got that when I was twenty-two."

Jordan shook her head. "You are such a mass of contradictions."

"Why do you say that?" He turned around to face her, bringing one leg up onto the bed.

Jordan touched the earrings at his left ear. "These and the tattoo scream heavy rocker... But you aren't a big partyer, are you?"

"Oh, I do the rocker thing," he said, smiling lopsidedly. "I just don't feel that being a rocker has to mean fucking anything that moves, or getting drunk and stupid in public."

Jordan knew what he meant. There were rockers, like Brenden and even her sometimes, that were legendary for their binges and excesses.

"Was that aimed at me, Mr. Silver?" she asked mildly, raising an eyebrow at him.

"Not at all," he replied without a trace of insincerity. "That was aimed at the ones who go onstage too drunk to perform, or tear up hotel rooms in drug-induced rages, or mistreat women solely on the basis that they're famous and can get away with it."

Jordan gazed at him for a long moment, wondering if this man would ever cease to surprise her.

"So you cook?" she asked finally.

"Yeah. Don't you?"

"Uh, no," she said, shaking her head with a grin.

"Well, good thing one of us does, isn't it?" he asked, getting up and reaching for his pants.

"Hey, I know every restaurant in L.A. that delivers twenty-four hours a day," she said with a laugh.

They spent the next two hours in her kitchen. She sat on the counter while he chopped vegetables, cut up meat, and selected seasonings.

"So, can I ask you a question?" she asked as he picked out wine and poured them both a glass.

"Sure," he said, leaning on the island across from where she sat.

"Do you make love to your wife the way you do other women?"

Dylan was silent, taking a drink of his wine. Then he shook his head. "No, I don't."

"Why?" she asked, thinking that maybe if he did, she wouldn't be such a bitch all the time.

Dylan blew his breath out with a shrug. "I don't find her at all attractive."

Jordan canted her head to the side, trying to figure that one out. "I saw her picture. She's pretty."

"She's pretty, yes," he agreed. "Outwardly. But inside, she's become very ugly over the years. And I've had the opportunity to see her in her full glory."

"Most men don't care about what's inside," Jordan said, her tone acerbic.

"Then there are plenty of women out there for them."

Jordan smiled. She liked that she was included in the half that was considered pretty on the inside too.

Later they sat eating in her living room, with a fire going in the fireplace.

"Okay, you're so hired," Jordan told him when she took her first spoonful of the soup he'd made.

"Am I?" he asked, grinning.

"Where did you learn to cook like this?" There wasn't an end to the sides of this man.

Dylan shrugged. "Just picked it up over the years. I can only handle chef-prepared food for so long. Sometimes I just need something simple."

Jordan nodded. That really did fit him. He had the feel of a man so comfortable in his own skin. He didn't seem to seek or even desire the acceptance of others. He was happy being himself.

They talked while they ate. Dylan finished eating before she did, and moved to sit next to the fire, wearing only his pants. Jordan set down her bowl and sat behind him. She was finding herself more and more attracted to him. Her hands slid up his chest, and she leaned forward to kiss his shoulder. He took her hands in his and lifted them to his lips, kissing each one. Jordan pressed closer to him, feeling warmth start inside her again.

They made love in front of the fireplace, then again in the kitchen when they took the dishes in, in the shower, and again in her bed. It was five a.m. before they finished. Jordan was sure she'd sleep for a week.

Dylan left her house at six a.m., kissing her on the lips and telling her he'd call her later. She rolled over onto her stomach and promptly fell asleep, sleeping until well after three that afternoon. She got up and ate some of the soup he'd made, then crawled back into bed feeling sated, relaxed, and damned good. Finally! An affair to enjoy without a hassle. And, God, he was so good in bed. Perfect.

♫   **Two**   ♫

Well, it was perfect… until she didn't hear from him for three days. Her mind started telling her *You've been used, idiot,* or *How easy was that for him? Second time he saw you…* and, finally *A notch on some rocker's bedpost!*

By the second day, she'd given in and tried his cell phone number. His voicemail picked up; she hung up without leaving a message. Why leave a message? What would she say?

"Uh, yeah, this is Jordan, remember me? You squeezed me in between Alyssa Milano and Maggie Turner?" No way. Not her style.

By the third day she was back to being angry at him. By that night, she'd decided that she'd been stupid and wouldn't be stupid ever again. She was lying in bed, listening to Nickelback; the song "Do This Anymore" was on. The bridge said exactly what she was thinking. When was she ever going to learn about men and their ways?

She didn't hear Dylan come in. She didn't see him stand there watching her singing the words to the song. She didn't notice him until he stepped forward, his eyes on her. She jumped.

"Fuck!" Her heart leaped into her throat. "How did you get in here?'

"Your maid." His eyes searched her face as he walked toward the bed.

Jordan sat up, steeling herself. "Look," she began, ready to give him the speech she'd been rehearsing in her head for the last few hours.

He reached out and touched her hand. She pulled it away, giving him a narrowed look. His face remained, as always, impassive.

"I've been thinking about it," she continued, "and I think we should keep this professional. I mean, it's always a bad idea to—"

"Jordan," he said, cutting her off, his voice strong but calm. "I'm sorry I didn't call you. When I got home, Marissa blew a gasket. She's been yelling for literally three days."

Jordan sensed that he was telling her the truth. From everything she'd read about Marissa Silver, and from hearing the woman on the phone with him, she knew he was being honest.

He cupped her face, his thumb smoothing over her cheek and his silver-gray eyes staring into hers. "I'm sorry."

She didn't know how to react. She knew she needed to be strong and tell him that this just wasn't going to work. It wasn't like it was a relationship—it was sex, albeit incredible, mind-blowing sex. He was married, for God's sake! She started to shake her head, trying to formulate a way to tell him no... His lips touched hers then, and there was no more talking, except when she got his shirt off and saw a dark black-and-blue bruise on the front of his shoulder.

"What happened?" She gasped at how dark the bruise was against his tanned skin.

"Transient flying object," he said, bending to kiss her again, forestalling any more questions.

He apologized with his body, in exquisite, sensual ways, making her willing to do anything, forgive anything, say anything to keep him coming back. Dylan took his time, appreciating every inch of her golden skin.

"God, you are so incredibly beautiful..." he whispered huskily, his lips on her neck.

Jordan arched against him, moaning out loud as his lips moved lower. His hands touched her, making her writhe, pressing closer. When she reached her release, she cried out his name over and over again. She'd orgasmed no less than ten times in the last four hours. She was exhausted, but when he continued to touch her, she moaned again and pulled him up her body, wanting him inside her. He slid inside her, and she shuddered at the sheer erotic feeling. She held on to him, letting him take them both to wondrous heights, yet again.

Afterwards they lay together, panting, sweating, and feeling extremely sated. Jordan lay on her back, Dylan half over her, his hand still on her waist. Jordan was just drifting off to sleep when Dylan's head came off the pillow. She opened her eyes, wondering what had startled him. He wasn't looking around him; he seemed to be looking inward. After a few moments, however, he did start to look around.

"Didn't I see a laptop in here last time I was here?"

"Yeah," she said, thinking he was crazy. "It's next to that desk." She pointed to the desk across the room.

Dylan got out of bed, his long, lithe body fantastic in the moonlight shining through the windows. Jordan turned over onto her stomach and watched him. He kneeled down, pulled out the laptop case, and took out the square machine.

"Is it charged?"

"I think so."

He stood and carried the laptop to the bed. Sitting down, his back to the headboard, he pulled the blankets up to his waist and set the laptop on his lap, opening it and turning it on. Jordan turned onto her side, angling her head so she could see what he was doing. Within minutes, his fingers were flying across the keys, putting down the lyrics to the song that had gone through his head. Jordan watched in awe. The words just flowed out of him without hesitation... It was amazing.

When he was done, Jordan sat up and looked at what he'd written, reading it over to herself. She glanced at Dylan; he had a very satisfied look on his face.

"You do this kind of thing often?" she asked.

"Only when I'm inspired."

"Is that often?"

"Not until lately," he said, his eyes looking directly into hers.

Jordan stared back at him, feeling the importance of what he'd just said. She was inspiring him again? Is that why Project had been tapped out?

Dylan watched her face. Seeing the question in her eyes, he nodded slowly. "I couldn't write anymore," he said softly. "There was nothing left to write about that anyone wanted to hear."

Jordan blinked a few times, surprised at how sad that made her feel. She kissed his lips, wanting to make him feel her empathy. His hands slid up her body to cup her face, his thumbs brushing her cheeks as they kissed. It was his way of accepting her understanding. They kissed for a few minutes, then he reached down and saved the song he'd just written, then set aside the laptop. Pulling her into his arms and kissing her again, he made love to her once more. It was a long but enjoyable night for both of them.

****

It ended up being the formula for the way Jordan Tate's third album was written. In bed, naked together, with a laptop and a great deal of lovemaking. Dylan loaded a songwriting program on her laptop, one that would allow them to map out the music for each song they'd written. Within a month, they had all the songs for the album written. The songs were passion-inspired, and reflected that in the words and music. It was something of a departure from Jordan's usual style, but she felt she was ready for a change.

Jordan called Brenden to let him know that she was ready to go back into the studio.

"You're sure?" Brenden asked.

"Dylan and I have twelve songs that are going to blow you away, Beege," Jordan said triumphantly.

"Well, let's see what you've got," Brenden said. "Meet me in the studio this morning at ten."

Jordan was there, on time for once. She handed Brenden the sheets of music with lyrics printed above the lines of musical notes. Brenden read them over one by one, looking more and more amazed by the minute.

"Damn..." he finally said as he set aside the sheets and looked at Jordan. "You two wrote all of these?"

Jordan nodded, looking extremely happy.

"I think you've probably got an entire album of hits there," he said, gesturing at the papers. "Go ahead and set your studio schedule. I'll approve it." He reached out and hugged her close. "It's good to have you back," he said softly.

Jordan gave him an extra squeeze. She knew she couldn't tell him about she and Dylan sleeping together. Brenden would probably lecture her for hours about the insanity of sleeping with a married man. So she kept silent about this new aspect of her life.

The time in the studio went well. Jordan was still feeling happy about producing something good again. She also found that, in the studio, Dylan was a total professional. Always on time, always ready to work. Whenever there was a question on how something should be played, he put in his suggestions, but never became irritated when his suggestion wasn't used. Jordan did find out that Dylan could play not only bass guitar, but lead and rhythm as well. He was able to help the guitarist come up with riffs that would fit the music he and Jordan had written. And when the rhythm guitarist was sick for a week, Dylan was able to take over from him and keep them moving forward on the album.

Jordan was thrilled with the way the album was going. They worked on it from eight in the morning until often nine at night.

Then she and Dylan would stay until midnight or so, listening to what they'd done that day and discussing what they wanted to rework. It was a complete collaboration between the two of them.

Brenden came in during many of the vocal sections and worked with Jordan to get the best performance out of her. Dylan sat back, amazed by Jordan's range. Her voice was as beautiful as she was. Brenden, being the incredible singer that he was, was able to get Jordan to stretch her voice, hit higher notes, hold them longer. They worked well together; that much was obvious.

Like most of the world, Dylan knew about Jordan and Brenden's on and off relationship. He found himself feeling a little bit jealous at seeing them relating so intimately. He also knew he had absolutely no right to be jealous—he was a married man. It was easy for Dylan to see why men like BJ Sparks, Joe Sinclair, and any number of others were drawn in by Jordan. She had a way about her that made you want to be around her. Everything about her said sexuality. And having known her quite intimately made it even more apparent. He recognized certain smiles, certain looks and gestures... They were how she made love. Dylan knew Jordan was different than any other woman he'd been with. He didn't know what it meant, but he was ready to let things happen they way they should. He was a firm believer in fate.

***

In three months, the album was within weeks of being completed. Brenden told Jordan that he'd rescheduled five shows that had been canceled during her last tour for two weeks from then. A few of the cancellations were because one of Joe's close friends had been shot, and since Joe had needed to be there, Jordan had felt like she did too. It had cost her money, and it had made her cancel three shows. There had been a couple of other incidents that had caused cancellations too. Now Jordan needed to do them. It was good timing, since the album was almost done and they needed to perform as a band since adding Dylan to the line-up.

Things were also getting difficult with Jordan and Dylan. Marissa was apparently very suspicious of the late nights Dylan spent with Jordan writing... and she became more so after the writing was done and they were spending a lot of time in the studio. They'd often leave the studio together and go to her house for a few hours before he went home. Jordan was getting to the point where she didn't want him to leave, and she knew that was going to be a problem. Suddenly the idea of sleeping with a married man wasn't so pleasant. She wanted him to be with her whenever she wanted him there, which lately was all the time.

One day, they wrapped up the studio time early, and Jordan and Dylan went and had dinner in a quiet restaurant. They managed to avoid the paparazzi by going up the coast a bit. Things were getting more difficult in that arena too: the paparazzi smelled an affair, and they wanted pictures of it. So far they'd only gotten photos of Jordan and Dylan in totally innocent-looking situations. But they were getting closer and sneakier.

After lingering over wine and talking for a long while, Dylan drove them back to Jordan's house. They spent hours making love, and talking in between. The conversations centered on the album and the tour. At three in the morning they both lay sleeping in her bed. A phone rang; Jordan stirred, glancing around.

"Dylan?" She nudged his shoulder. "I think that's your phone."

"Mmm?" he murmured, then sat up, rubbing his eyes and reaching for his cell phone.

He picked up his phone and lay back on the bed, still looking tired. "Hello?"

He was blasted the second she heard him on the other end.

"Where the bloody fucking hell are you?" Marissa screeched.

Dylan was fully awake now, glancing at the clock and grimacing.

"Well?"

"I'm working," he replied mildly.

"Like hell you are. You're fucking her, aren't you? You bloody bastard!" she yelled.

"I'll be home in a while," he said, as if she hadn't just screamed at him.

"You'll come home right now!"

"I'll get home when I'm done," he answered, his voice still calm.

"Yes, Dylan, when you're done fucking her, you can come home, and I'll fucking kill you for making me look like a fool!" Marissa screamed, then slammed down the phone.

Dylan looked at the phone, his grin wry. "Bye then," he said, hitting the End button.

Jordan was fully awake by then, having heard some of Marissa's words.

"She's mad," Jordan said, unnecessarily.

"You think so?" Dylan asked, still grinning.

"Dylan..." Jordan said. "She said she'd kill you. Was she serious?"

"Jordan, she threatens to kill me often." He didn't sound the least bit worried.

Jordan stared at him, trying to gage if he was serious or not. "She's going to scream at you for days again, isn't she?"

Dylan expelled a deep breath. "Probably."

"Shit," Jordan said, disappointed. "That means I won't get to see you for a while."

"It'll give you time to redecorate." He winked.

"Not funny," she said sourly.

"Sorry," he replied, still looking playful.

Jordan saw it and sighed. "I'm sorry, I know it's not your fault." She put her hand to his cheek. "I just like having you here."

"Well, we'll get five nights in a row in two weeks," he said. "And then there'll be the tour for the album..."

"Mmm… heaven," she said, smiling.

"I better get going." He leaned over to kiss her lips softly.

"I know." She nodded, doing her best not to beg him not to go.

She watched him dress, having to bite her lip to keep from asking him not to leave. She didn't like the way Marissa had sounded—she'd sounded crazy. Jordan kept telling herself that Dylan knew his wife, and he wasn't worried, so why should she be?

He left a half hour later, taking his time to kiss her deeply, which only made her long for him again.

The next day, he didn't show up to the studio. He called and left a message at the studio offices saying he would be out for a couple of days. It was very businesslike, and Jordan was sure it was because Marissa was watching his every move. Jordan didn't hear from him at all either. She wasn't sure what that meant, but she refused to get upset at him. She knew that's what Marissa was probably counting on. If Dylan's mistress turned into a shrew like his wife, he'd probably break it off. Why keep sleeping with someone that was just as bad as his wife?

After three days, however, Jordan's resolve was wavering. She'd called his cell phone a couple of times, ready to hang up if Marissa answered. She knew her phone number wouldn't appear on his cell phone, because she had a private number that wouldn't show up on the display. Both times she got a message that said "This number is unavailable at this time." She wasn't sure what that meant.

***

Meanwhile, in the Silver home, things were flying, literally. So far Marissa had cleared the kitchen counter, throwing ceramic canisters, pots, pans, and the two Imari plates that sat on the counter as decoration. Dylan blocked it all, side-stepping the flying pans.

He actually caught the Imari plates; they were antiques. He set them up on top of the cabinets where Marissa couldn't reach, looking back at her mildly, his usual wry grin on his lips.

He looked around him. There was flour, sugar, coffee, rice, and brown sugar all over the floor. There were broken pieces of pottery and glass too. He shook his head; the housekeeper was not going to be pleased. Gingerly stepping over the debris, he walked out of the kitchen.

Marissa stared after him, thinking that killing him did sound like an option right now. With that thought in mind, she pulled out one of the carving knives from its block in the cupboard. She walked into the other room, finding him in his den, his feet up on the coffee table, a sheaf of papers in hand as he read them over.

Anger overwhelmed her. How dare he look so fucking calm! Without stopping to think, she threw the knife at him. He had the temerity to look shocked for a moment. He also had amazing re-action time, because he threw himself to the side, narrowly avoiding being hit by the hurled blade. But Marissa wasn't done. Seeing that her first attack failed, she launched herself at him. Her nails raked at him, catching him on the throat and face before he managed to grab her hands.

"This is getting beyond ridiculous now," he said, still annoyingly placid. He turned her around so she had her back to him, his arms holding her tight. "Are you done?"

"Let go of me, you bastard!" she screeched.

"I'll take that as a no," he replied, his voice right next to her ear.

"Let go!"

"Calm down, and I shall." His voice was the epitome of serenity.

"Dylan let me go!" she yelled, struggling against his hold.

Dylan merely sat there, holding her, refusing to let go, until she finally calmed down and relaxed against him.

"I hate you," she said defeatedly.

"I'm sorry to hear that." Dylan let her go.

She jumped away from him and turned to look at him, her brown eyes searching his face. She grinned with satisfaction to see that she'd drawn blood on his cheek and neck.

"I know you're fucking her, Dylan," she said, her tone grating. "And when I have proof, I swear to you, I'll kill you. So you'd better stop seeing her. Do you understand me?"

Dylan looked back at her impassively. He knew not to provoke her further. He also refused to deny anything; he wasn't going to lie. He merely remained silent, his silver-gray eyes staring at her unemotionally. Marissa picked up his cell phone and threw it at him. He ducked and it hit the wall behind him, smashing into pieces. He glanced back at the remains of his cell phone, then back at Marissa. She stormed out of the room.

After she was gone, he glanced to his side and saw the hole in the couch where the knife had struck. He picked up the knife and looked at it, flipping it in his hand so he held it by the knife point. He whipped his arm back and threw it. The point stuck into the door of his den. Only then did he release his pent-up breath, leaning back against the couch. Marissa was getting more and more violent.

Normally when she'd get this riled up over a woman she suspected he was seeing, he'd back off the affair. But this time was different. He didn't want to stop seeing Jordan. She was the inspiration he'd been needing. Jordan gave him back the life that had been run out of him by his wife. It wasn't that he couldn't handle Marissa—there were a lot of things he could have done to fight back, but it just wasn't his way. Things with her had never been ideal, but there were things in the past that he was responsible for, disappointments Marissa had withstood, that she now held over him. They didn't have kids because Marissa had two miscarriages. She blamed both on Dylan, claiming that she'd been so upset with his screwing around that she'd lost the babies.

Dylan didn't totally believe that, but part of him felt guilty. It was that part of him that had kept him with her for years. And he'd continue to stay with her, but he wasn't going to stop seeing Jordan.

Later that night, he knocked on Jordan's door. She answered it and gasped.

"Oh my God, Dylan!" she exclaimed, reaching up to touch the scratches on his face.

"It's okay," he assured her, even as she pulled him into the foyer so she could see the scratches better.

Her fingers lightly traced the scratches. She pulled aside his shirt collar to see the ones on his neck.

"That bitch!" she said in anger, her eyes going to his. "She did this because of me, didn't she?"

"She did this because she has absolutely no control over her temper." Dylan took off his jacket and hung it in the closet.

"And she lost her temper because of me," Jordan said, moving into his arms.

"Honey," he said, hugging her to him, "don't blame yourself, okay? This is my problem, and I'll deal with it. It's okay."

Jordan rubbed her face against his shirt. Dylan smiled fondly and touched her under the chin, lifting her face to his. He kissed her, his hands touching her face.

They ended up in her bedroom once again, making love. Afterwards they talked.

"Does she know about your affairs?" Jordan asked as she lay in his arms.

Dylan shrugged. "I'm very discreet about what I do, not to the point of cloak and dagger, but I do my best to keep it out of the public eye."

"But has she ever caught you?"

"She's gotten to the point where she's been convinced before," he said.

"And what happened then?" She turned her head to look up at him.

Dylan took a breath and blew it out. He put his arm up, turning his forearm toward her. "This."

Jordan saw the three- to four-inch scar on his arm. "Oh Jesus, Dylan, what did she do?" she asked, touching the scar.

"Butcher knife," he said. "She was going for my chest. I blocked it."

"Damn…" She grimaced. "She really has anger management issues, doesn't she?"

"You could say that," Dylan said, his voice somber.

"Should you even be here?" she asked him, worried suddenly. "I mean, here with me, is this safe for you?"

"I want to be here with you, Jordan." His hand slid up to touch her hand that rested on his arm.

She nodded, smiling at him, but the worry didn't leave her eyes. He kissed her softly on the lips. Later that evening when he left, Jordan had to force herself not to beg him not to leave. She was worried about him now.

She walked him to the door. There she turned to him, putting her head against his chest and hugging him. Dylan smiled and hugged her close, feeling a rush of affection for the concern she was showing. It felt good to have someone worry about him again.

Jordan lifted her face and looked up at him, her gold eyes almost bronze in the light of the foyer. "I can't lose you, Dylan," she said softly.

"You aren't going to lose me, Jordan." Leaning down, he kissed her lips, his hands cupping her face gently. "A week and a half, babe, and we're out of here for five nights together, okay?"

Jordan nodded, letting her breath out slowly. He left, kissing her quickly on the lips again.

***

She didn't see him again for days. They had stopped working in the studio, giving the sound man and the producer time to work on what they'd already done. So it was more difficult for Dylan to get away to see Jordan. Within the week and a half, Jordan only saw him twice, and even those were short visits. He told her that Marissa was on the warpath, watching his every move. It irritated Jordan no end. How dare she! It was public knowledge that Marissa Silver slept around—how dare she act like Dylan had no right to do the same?

Jordan found that she missed him a lot. He'd become this calming influence in her life. Grounding her in a way she'd never experienced before. She knew he was starting to get to her, and it bothered her. He'd never said he'd leave his wife, and she'd never asked him to. It was a physical relationship; that was it. Right? Wasn't it? She knew that it felt so good to be with him, and when they talked, she felt like they totally clicked. He had different views and thoughts on things, but he was never condescending about it.

If he thought something different from her, he merely explained how he saw it. Jordan would do the same. He'd ask her a few questions about her views, and she found herself doing the same. "It isn't that either of us is wrong, Jordan," he'd told her. "It's that we both have different experiences to draw from. That's what shapes our views. When we share our experiences, that sometimes changes our views." He was always sensible, and never angry or cold. She'd never met such a warm-hearted man; she'd always assumed men like Dylan would be wimps. But nothing about Dylan was the least bit wimpy. He was a strong, intelligent man.

When the day came for them to leave on the trip, Jordan was anxious to get to the airport where the Badlands jet waited for them. She was anxious to see Dylan. She arrived twenty minutes early, putting her stuff in the one bedroom on the plane. Everyone else would put their stuff in the areas in the forward part of the roomy plane. Jordan took advantage of the fact that she was the star in the band. She was determined to have time alone with Dylan. Their first show was in Rockford, Illinois, so it was going to be a long flight. Jordan intended to spend that time with him.

Brenden arrived to see them off. Jordan went down to talk to him. He left a little while later, saying he had a meeting to get to. She hugged him and thanked him for the use of the jet. Since their five concerts were spread out, the jet made it much easier. She appreciated that Brenden would give up his plane for five nights. Brenden appreciated that Jordan hadn't balked at doing five shows in five nights. It wasn't like her at all.

Jordan was still standing on the tarmac when Dylan's Jaguar drove into the area. Jordan didn't realize that there was someone else in the car with Dylan until he stopped. That's when Jordan saw her. Marissa. She was a pert-looking blonde, with dark eyes and a nasty slant to her mouth. It was obvious the woman was so used to being a bitch she didn't know how to turn it off.

Marissa narrowed her eyes at Jordan and shot a look over at Dylan. As expected, Dylan didn't react in the slightest. In fact, he quirked his lips at Jordan, showing that he knew he was only further irritating his wife. He walked to the back of the car, opened the trunk, and pulled out his bags, including his bass. Setting one of his bags down, he handed Marissa the keys, saying something to her that caused her to glare at him. Then he walked toward the plane.

Marissa called his name, running to catch up to him, his long-legged strides carrying him much farther than hers did. While Jordan looked up, Marissa moved to stand in front of him. She grabbed a handful of his shirt and drew his head down to hers, kissing him passionately on the lips. Dylan held his bags, obviously enduring the kiss but not impressed by it. When Marissa let him go, she turned to look at Jordan, standing in front of Dylan.

"He's married, you do know that, right?" Marissa said, her tone antagonistic.

"Completely," Jordan replied, her gold eyes challenging.

"You bitch!" Marissa screeched. She started toward Jordan.

That's when Dylan interceded. "Marissa," he said smoothly, stepping into her path. "Let's not have a scene here, okay?"

"You're protecting her?" Marissa asked, her voice dangerously low.

"She's paying my salary," Dylan said simply.

"And you're fucking her for it."

Dylan said nothing, his face impassive. He didn't move, and Marissa knew this wasn't the place to cause a scene.

"You'll pay for this," she growled, whirling and walking away from him.

"Nice…" Jordan said from behind him.

Dylan didn't reply, watching Marissa storm over to the Jaguar and get in. He winced as she squealed the tires when she left the tarmac.

"How do I know I'm going to be paying for it with my car?" he asked, a grin on his lips as he turned to Jordan.

"I'll pay for it if she does any damage," she said contritely. "I'm sorry. She got to me."

Dylan shrugged. "Not to worry, I have insurance." He gave her a quick kiss. "Ready to go?"

"We're the only ones who made it on time," she said, smiling.

"Well, that's a shame…" he said with a smirk.

She took his hand, pulling him up the stairs to the plane and then to the back, where Brenden's personal cabin was located. She dragged him inside, locked the door, and basically attacked him, throwing him on the bed. He laughed at her zeal and sat up, kissing her. She wrapped her arms around his neck, pressing closer to him.

When the Badlands jet took off, they were making love, and they didn't bother coming out until the plane landed at

Chicago/Rockford International Airport. The rest of the band, of course, knew what was going on. None of them were surprised, since Jordan often had her men on the bus or plane with them, and she rarely surfaced for air. The one thing the band worried about was that when Jordan dumped this guy, they'd be out a bassist again.

The sound check at the Rockford MetroCentre went much smoother than any of the band had anticipated, even though there were a ton of problems with the sound. When Jordan had received screeching feedback for the fifth time in twenty minutes, it was obvious she was losing her temper. The band was waiting for the usual explosion.

Dylan walked over to her. "Slow deep breaths, honey. They're working on it..." he said softly.

Jordan glanced at him. His silver-gray eyes looked directly into hers. She took a deep breath and expelled it slowly, nodding her head. Dylan smiled at her, then walked away. The rest of the band looked on in awe, glancing at each other and shrugging. Whatever this guy had, it was certainly working wonders on the ever-temperamental singer.

When the sound check was over, they all went back to the hotel. They had four hours until they needed to be back. Jordan was her usual restless self before a show. Dylan watched her pace back and forth in the hotel room. He sat on the couch in the living area of the suite Jordan had been given, his feet up on the coffee table.

Jordan glanced at him and saw the ever-amused look on his face. Stopping, she glared at him.

"Don't you ever get keyed up?" she asked, her tone almost accusing.

Dylan thought about it for a moment, then shook his head. "Not anymore, no."

"Because it's not your band?"

"Nah." He shrugged. "I haven't gotten edgy in years. I consider it a waste of energy."

Jordan made a face at him, then went back to pacing. Dylan watched her. She was going to be exhausted before they ever even got to the show. He got up and stood in her path. She stopped, giving him a narrowed look. He smiled engagingly, then he slid his hand under her hair, pulling her to him and kissing her lips.

She laughed as he kissed her. "What are you doing?"

"I figure if you're going to waste energy, I can at least give you a better outlet." he said, grinning.

"Ohhhh..." she said, widening her eyes and grinning too.

They ended up on the couch, making out like teenagers. He didn't make love to her, knowing that if they got into all that, they would indeed be exhausted for the show. He did, however, get her feeling very calm and very centered for the performance.

The show went off without a hitch, and everyone was thrilled with the way it went. That night, back at the hotel, Jordan and Dylan made love for hours again, still on the adrenaline high from the show. They ordered room service at three a.m.

"God, we need to get some sleep," he said, rubbing his eyes.

"Why?" Jordan asked with a smile.

"Because we have a plane to catch in the morning."

"Are you ever late?" she asked, knowing he probably never was.

"There's the occasional tardiness."

"Oh yeah?" she asked cynically.

"Yeah," he replied, leaning over to kiss her.

She grinned, kissing him back.

She lay in bed later that morning, thinking along those lines. She was almost always late. People thought it was because she always wanted to make an entrance, but the fact of the matter was she simply had no grasp of time management. She was forever over-booking herself, thinking she could get it all done, and then finding that there was no way she could. She never seemed to learn from her mistakes either. She was just always late; it was a fact.

Hell, if anything, the only thing in her life that was always on time was her period... That's when it hit her. She was late... Oh shit! That's all her brain screamed to her as the thought hit. Sliding out from under Dylan's arm, she got out of bed and reached for her purse. She found her date book and went back over the dates circled neatly in red, one of the few things she was careful about. And there it was—she was two weeks late. She was *never* late, and she was two weeks late. Oh shit.

Jordan sat down on the toilet in the hotel bathroom and stared at the book in her hands, unable to believe this. Finally she'd met a man she could have a good friendship and a sexual relationship with. Someone she really felt was a good influence on her, and what happened? It got screwed up by her getting pregnant!

"Great, Jordan, just great," she muttered to herself.

She had no idea how Dylan would react. Surely, he'd be pissed. Obviously he didn't want children—he and his wife of eighteen years didn't have kids. How stupid could she be? She had birth control pills; she took them all the time. But being with Dylan was such a consuming thing that she knew there were times when she'd missed. She hadn't done so intentionally, and had doubled up the next day like you were supposed to. There had been days, however, when she didn't remember if she'd taken it the day before, or if it had been two days.

"Shit, shit, shit..." she chanted to herself. This was going to screw everything up.

Dylan would go running back to the safety of his wife, and Jordan would be on her own and pregnant. Did she really want him to stay? He was a great guy, and much more than she'd thought originally. He was brilliant, handsome, funny, intelligent... and *married, Jordan, married*! He'd never left his wife for any of the other women he'd slept with. What made her any different? Nothing, except that she'd just fucked up and gotten pregnant. *Oh yes, have to be unique, don't you, Jordan?*

The next couple of days were disastrous. Jordan was so irritated at herself that it came out in everything that she did. She had never handled anger well, and this time was no different. She ended up screaming at everyone, even Dylan, who simply looked back at her calmly. She began to see what drove Marissa Silver so crazy. When she screamed at him, he didn't react. There was no sign that he was taking her seriously. Fact of the matter was, he shouldn't take her seriously, since her anger wasn't really at him.

There were a number of incidents, starting with the plane the next morning; it wasn't ready to go when everyone got there. Jordan threw a fit. The next venue was a smaller one, and the sound equipment once again wasn't up to par. Dylan hung back and let Jordan vent her rage, sensing it was something she needed to do. When she got to the point of it becoming physical, however, he intervened and calmed her down.

That first night after the show, Dylan went to the room that had been reserved for him. He'd called ahead and had his bags moved from Jordan's room to the other one. He wasn't sure what had set Jordan off, but he felt she needed some space to herself. If she asked him to come to her room he would, but he wasn't going to assume she wanted him there.

By the fourth night, Jordan was fed up with being handled with kid gloves. She was pissed that Dylan had abandoned her when this was supposed to be their time together. In the back of her mind, she knew she was the cause, but she didn't want to acknowledge that just yet. Instead she stormed to the room he'd taken, pounding on the door until he opened it.

He was wearing faded jeans and a black cotton tunic-style shirt. He smiled warmly on seeing her at his door. She gave him a sour look and moved past him, glancing around as she did. Part of her expected to find another woman in the room. She was relieved when she didn't.

"Why did you take another room?" she asked sharply.

Dylan looked back at her, his face the picture of serenity. Finally he shrugged. "I just figured you could use some space." He sat down on the bed.

"I see," she said, still sounding angry.

She started pacing. Dylan watched her for a few moments.

"Jordan," he said cautiously, "what's wrong?"

"Nothing," she snapped, far too quickly.

Dylan nodded slowly, still watching her pace. "Okay, so you don't want to talk about it." He didn't sound offended, angry, or even put out.

"There's nothing to talk about, Dylan," she said, turning to him and putting her hands on her hips. "I said there's nothing wrong."

Again Dylan nodded, an amused light in his eyes. "Okay, so you're very tense."

"Right." She walked over to the bar and reached for the Southern Comfort.

Then she realized that she couldn't drink, because if she decided to keep the baby, it would hurt it.

"Damn it," she said, slamming the bottle down on the bar.

Dylan got up and walked over to her. Her back was to him. Standing behind her, he slid his hands over her shoulders, his thumbs massaging the muscles in her back.

"Baby, you are so tense..." he said softly, his hands continuing to massage her gently.

"Dylan..." she began, her tone between irritated and cautionary.

"It's okay, babe," he said soothingly. "You don't have to talk to me, okay? I just want you to relax. We don't have to talk at all. Just relax..." he continued, as his hands massaged away the tension in her back, neck, and arms.

Jordan sighed and leaned against the bar, letting him relax her. After a few minutes, he took her hand and led her over to the bed, pulling her down on it beside him. He lay on his side, turning her to face him, and continued to massage her. She kicked off her shoes.

"Just relax, babe," he said. "Take slow breaths… and let the tension leave your body… Don't try to think about your problems… Problems never get solved by looking at them constantly. Just let it go for now… let it go…"

Within a half hour, Jordan was so relaxed she was falling asleep.

"Haven't slept much, have you?" he asked softly.

She shook her head.

"Well, sleep now, baby." He kissed her temple. "You need your rest."

Jordan snuggled against his warmth and allowed herself to sleep.

Dylan held her all night. Jordan woke the next morning feeling so refreshed it was amazing to her. She opened her eyes. He was still asleep. She stared up at him, thinking about the way he'd handled her the night before. She'd been breathing serious fire, and he simply got around that. He hadn't raised his voice; he hadn't retreated into cold silence. In the end, he'd allowed her the anger she was feeling, without taking anything away from her or taking it personally. Dylan Silver was an amazing man, and he was what she needed.

Dylan stirred, his gray eyes looking silver in the morning light streaming through the windows.

"Good morning," he said, his smile warm.

Jordan bit her lip, her eyes staring up into his. "It is now," she said, kissing him softly on the lips. "Dylan, I'm sorry. I've been taking things out on you, and it's not your fault. I'm really—"

His fingers on her lips stopped her. "It's okay, babe," he said. "I know you aren't mad at me. I just wish you'd talk to me, so I could maybe help you through what you are mad about."

For one crazy second, Jordan wanted to tell him about being pregnant, but she vetoed the idea just as quickly. She wasn't sure what she wanted to do, and the last thing she wanted was to run him off. She'd been thinking that maybe she'd get a nice quiet little abortion, and he'd never know about the baby. But she hadn't made a decision yet. Telling him now might ruin everything before it was even necessary.

"I can't right now," she said softly, her eyes indicating that she was sorry for shutting him out.

Dylan nodded, not looking offended or angry. "I'm here when and if you can, okay?"

"Okay."

They got up and got dressed, meeting the plane on time. The rest of the band was relieved to see they'd apparently solved whatever Jordan's issue was. That night, the concert in Las Vegas went great. The crowd was loud and boisterous. Jordan was on a high again. As usual, Dylan hung back, letting her enjoy herself.

After the show, Jordan told Dylan she was going to head to the hotel. Dylan kissed her and said he'd be there soon. He'd gotten caught up in a long conversation with a contest winner about Project—she was a big fan. The young woman stared at Jordan as if in awe, then looked back at Dylan.

"Are you dating her?"

"We're friends," Dylan said, his smile sincere.

"Wow..." The young woman looked at him again, more curious about him now.

"I better get going," he said, wiping his brow with a towel. "I need a shower desperately."

The young woman canted her head to the side. "Guess you don't need any help with that, huh?"

"With what?" Dylan asked.

"Your shower," she said, giving him a wink.

"Uh, no." Dylan grinned to take the sting out of the rejection. "But thanks for the offer."

The girl looked disappointed, but nodded. Dylan left a few minutes later, knowing it was time to get out of there. When the "fans" were at the come-on stage, it was time to go.

***

Jordan walked out of the backstage door to find a whole host of cameras and lights in her face.

"Ms. Tate, how do you feel about Joe Sinclair now?" one reporter asked, shoving a microphone in her face.

"What?" Jordan asked, shocked that someone was asking a question about Joe now. Jesus, it had been almost nine months!

"Are you mad that he remarried his ex-wife?" another reporter yelled.

"Did you know he was here just last night having the ceremony?" another screamed.

Jordan stared at them in stunned silence. Joe had remarried Randy? Last night? Here? She felt sick suddenly. She didn't know why, but it hurt like hell to hear it from these vultures. She blindly moved past them, shoving them away from her when they crowded too close. Making it to the waiting car, she told the driver to "move it."

Brenden heard from the promoter that Jordan had been ambushed by reporters. He also heard what they'd told her. He knew she'd be hurting. Unfortunately, he couldn't get away, so he did the next best thing. He called the band, asking them to check on Jordan. They all told him that Dylan was the best candidate for that job. Brenden wasn't altogether sure what they meant by that, but he knew that Dylan did have a good effect on Jordan's moods. So he called Dylan.

Dylan answered his cell on the third ring, having just gotten to the hotel.

"Hello?" he said as he walked to the front desk to check for messages. There were two, both from Marissa.

"Dylan, it's Brenden."

"Hey, BJ, what's up?" Dylan rolled his eyes at the messages from Marissa and headed for the elevators.

"Can you do a quick check on Jordan for me?"

"Sure," Dylan said, thinking, *I'm going to see her in about ten minutes.*

"She got some shitty news tonight. I want to make sure she's okay."

"What news?" Dylan asked, surprised. She'd been perfectly happy when she'd left the show.

"She heard that Joe Sinclair remarried his ex-wife." Brenden was fairly sure that Dylan would already know about Joe. Hell, half the world knew about Joe.

"Oh…" Dylan grimaced. He'd already punched for the floor to his room, which was above Jordan's floor. He had to wait through a few people and floors to punch in a new number. "I'll head over to check on her right now."

"Great, man, thanks," Brenden said. "Tell her I'll be there later tonight if she needs me."

"Okay," Dylan said, already getting out of the elevator and striding down the hall to Jordan's room.

He hung up with Brenden and knocked on Jordan's door. She didn't answer. He waited a few minutes, knocking a couple more times. He headed down to the front desk and asked the girl at the desk if Jordan Tate had come back to the hotel. Yes she had, she told him with a shy smile. She recognized him; for once it was helpful.

"I don't suppose you could give me a key to her room?"

"Well, Mr. Silver, we're not supposed to do that…"

"Please, miss." Dylan touched her hand. "It's very important."

73

The girl glanced around and then punched up the codes to program another card for Jordan's room. She handed it to Dylan with a wink.

"Thanks," he said with a brilliant smile. "You're an angel."

The girl smiled back brightly.

Dylan headed to Jordan's room, opened the door, and stepped inside. He walked into the bedroom portion of the suite. She was sitting on the bed, staring at her hands, her head bowed, her hair falling in front of her face. Dylan watched her for a few moments and saw that tears were falling on her hands.

Stepping forward, he called her name softly.

Her head came up, and he could see tears streaming down her cheeks.

"Jordan..." he said, his tone pained as he walked toward her.

She shook her head. He paused, staring down at her.

She dropped her head again, looking at her hands. "You know that I used to hate being off stage," she said, her voice quiet and defeated. "But then I met Joe, and I didn't mind it so much. I actually got to the point where I couldn't wait to get off stage so I could be with him..." She raised her head. "Why wasn't I enough for him?" she asked, her voice so hurt that Dylan felt it. "Why aren't I enough for anyone? What's wrong with me?" Fresh tears streamed from her eyes.

Dylan sat down on the bed, pulling her into his arms. "Nothing is wrong with you, Jordan. Nothing."

She shook her head, leaning against him heavily. "I just don't understand..." she said, her voice ragged.

Dylan held her, letting her cry and doing his best to soothe her. He didn't know enough about Joe Sinclair to judge what had happened between them. When she'd calmed, she rested against him quietly.

"Tell me about him," Dylan said, sensing that she needed to talk right then.

Jordan told Dylan all about Joe. Eventually she told him about the fateful cruise where she'd asked Joe about ever remarrying or having kids.

"What did he say?"

"He said he already had two kids," she said. "And that no, he hadn't really thought about getting remarried..."

Dylan nodded. "And that hurt."

"I guess I felt like he was saying I wasn't enough to make him want to have more kids, to make him want to commit to someone again. I felt temporary."

"And you two broke up after that?"

"No, not right after that," Jordan said. "In fact, I was with him when he found out about a close friend of his being shot. But we just weren't the same after that. And eventually he broke up with me, telling me he couldn't give me what I needed."

"And he felt that was children and marriage?"

Jordan nodded. "I told him I didn't care, but..."

"But?" Dylan asked gently.

"But I think I was just trying to hold on to him," she said. "I wanted him to be the one I was meant for. But I think part of me always knew I wasn't. Randy, his wife, was who he was meant for. But that meant I didn't have anyone again. And I'm just so tired..."

"I know," Dylan said, hugging her. "The hardest thing in the world to be is alone."

Jordan nodded, feeling like he understood her. She looked up at him and saw the depth of caring in his eyes. He'd just spent the last two hours listening to her go on and on about another man. Here he was, holding her, commiserating with her. She reached up and kissed him. His hand cupped her cheek as he kissed her back. He used both thumbs to brush away the tears that were still wet on her cheeks, kissing her softly as he did. Jordan wrapped her arms around him and deepened the kiss. He responded in kind, allowing her to exorcise her grief on him. The lovemaking was, as usual, fantastic. Afterwards, she snuggled against him, feeling drained, but not nearly as dismal. At least one man wanted her. But how much? The thought nagged at her as she fell into an exhausted sleep.

The words "What the fuck?" muttered angrily in an English-accented voice, woke Jordan a few hours later. She recognized the voice as Brenden's. Turning over, she looked toward the doorway to the bedroom. He was standing in that doorway, staring at Dylan's bare back.

"Brenden... Just wait..." she said, getting out of bed and grabbing her bathrobe.

She could see by the look on Brenden's face he was about to explode, so she hurriedly tied the bathrobe while she ushered him back out into the living area of the suite. She quietly closed the bedroom door. Fortunately, since Brenden exploded a moment later.

"I'll fucking kill him!" he snarled, shocking Jordan.

"For what?"

"For taking advantage of you, that's what," Brenden said, his blue-green eyes fiery. "I asked him to check on you, that was all."

"Beege," Jordan said, shaking her head. "He didn't take advantage of me, okay?"

"Like hell he didn't!" Brenden raged. "You were upset, and he figured now was the time to put the moves on you, the bastard..."

"Uh, Beege," Jordan cut in. "Dylan and I have been sleeping together for over three months now."

"What?" Brenden asked, looking dumbstruck suddenly.

Jordan nodded. "Yeah, so he didn't take advantage of me, okay?"

Brenden stared at her for a full minute, his look going from shocked to puzzled to downright pissed off.

"Are you fucking crazy?"

"Huh?" Jordan wasn't sure how he'd made that leap.

"He's married, Jordan," he said. "Not getting-divorced married like Joe was, but bloody fucking married. Do you not get that?"

"I know he's married, Beege." Jordan sat down on the couch.

"So what's possessed you to sleep with him?" Brenden asked, his tone biting.

Jordan narrowed her eyes. "Who the hell are you to talk, Brenden? You were sleeping with Allexx when you knew she was married—did I hassle you?"

"As a matter of fact you did," Brenden countered hotly.

"I was pissed when she fucked you over, Brenden, hardly the same thing."

"All the same, Jordan, she wasn't known for sleeping around in Hollywood either. Dylan Silver sleeps with the highest-caliber women in town and has never even talked about leaving his wife for one of them."

"Who says I want him to leave his wife for me?" Jordan asked irritably. "You know, Brenden, I can just fuck a guy without it being a lifetime commitment."

"Can you?" Brenden asked, his voice sharp.

"Yeah, I can."

Brenden looked at her for a long moment, then shook his head. "Bullshit," he said. "Ever since Joe, you want the real deal. That's why you haven't dated anyone for more than ten minutes since you and Joe broke up."

"I'm not you, Brenden, okay?" Jordan said. "I don't need the real fucking deal. I had a taste of that and it hurt like hell. I don't want it again."

"Liar."

"Fuck you," Jordan growled.

"You're saying you don't have any feelings for Dylan?" Brenden asked, changing tactics.

Jordan gave him a stony look. "I like him. He's a nice guy."

"Fine," Brenden said. "Then leave with me tonight."

"What?" Jordan asked. "Why?"

"Because I want you where I can keep tabs on you," Brenden said. "This shit with Joe was unexpected, and I was worried about you. But now I'm more worried about what you're doing with Silver."

"I'm an adult, Brenden." Jordan shook her head.

"Then be smart," Brenden said. "He won't leave his wife for you. If he's just sex, you can get that anywhere with a lot less complication. If Marissa Silver finds out he's sleeping with you, she'll probably come after you with a bazooka. I don't need that right now with one of my artists."

"One of your artists?" Jordan raised an eyebrow at him.

"And my best friend," he replied, glowering.

Jordan leaned back against the couch. Brenden was right. Dylan would never leave Marissa for her. She already knew that… And now there was the baby. She looked at Brenden for a few moments, then finally nodded.

"Okay, I'll leave with you tonight."

"You will?"

"Yeah," she said, moving to stand. "Let me grab a few things. You can have the road manager get the rest of my stuff, okay?"

"Okay…" Brenden said cautiously. He was waiting for the other shoe to drop.

He watched as Jordan walked back into the room. She got dressed quietly. She grabbed a few things, stuffing them in a bag. She kneeled next to the bed and kissed Dylan softly on the cheek. Then she walked back out to where Brenden stood waiting. She left with him, closing the door to the room quietly.

Later, on the private plane back to Los Angeles, Jordan glanced over at Brenden. He was staring out the window, watching the landscape.

"Beege," she began.

"Hmm?"

"There's something I need to tell you." She put her hand up defensively. "But I need you to not go ballistic on me, okay?"

"What is it?" he asked, already looking cautious.

Jordan grimaced, knowing he was likely to blow a gasket. "I'm pregnant."

Brenden's mouth dropped open. "Are you serious?"

Jordan nodded, looking penitent.

Brenden shook his head. "Unbelievable."

Jordan was relieved that he didn't explode, but she wasn't sure what he was thinking. She stayed silent, letting him digest this latest news. It was a long short flight home.

***

Dylan woke the next morning in an empty bed. He turned over, rubbing his eyes, and looked around. It took him about ten minutes to figure out that Jordan wasn't in the suite. Two hours later, he found out she'd been escorted home by BJ Sparks himself. He took that news with a calm nod, but inside he was wondering exactly what that meant. He did know one thing—he needed to set something in motion. It was something he'd decided that morning before he'd fallen asleep with Jordan under him. He intended to see it through.

The flight back to L.A. was quiet. No one was sure what it meant that Jordan had left early. But they did notice that Dylan Silver didn't seem to mind at all. Things weren't always as they seemed.

♪ THREE ♪

Brenden drove his Lamborghini Diablo down the streets of Beverly Hills, glancing over at Jordan a number of times. She knew his excuse for getting out, needing orange juice and cigarettes immediately, was just that. He needed to exorcise his concern for her, and that's what he was doing. Driving his car at breakneck speeds in the wee hours of the morning when the streets were somewhat deserted.

"So what are you going to do?" he asked her finally.

Jordan knew he was talking about the baby. He knew she'd been hiding out at his house, trying to decide what to do about her pregnancy.

She let her breath out in a sigh, shaking her head. "I don't know, Beege."

"Do you want to keep the baby?"

She looked pensive for a moment, then nodded. "I thought at first I could just get an abortion, but this may be my last chance to have a baby, BJ, and I don't want to lose that."

"Okay," Brenden said, knowing that she'd wanted a baby for a while now. "But you know you're going to have to tell him, right?"

"Why?" she asked, looking worried.

"It's going to become a bit obvious, love."

"True, with the tour and all."

Brenden grimaced. "Well, that's not what I meant," he said, as he turned into the local twenty-four-hour grocery store.

"What did you mean?" she asked, narrowing her eyes at him.

Brenden pressed his lips together guiltily and got out of the car.

"Brenden?" Jordan got out of the car too and looked across at him. "What did you do?"

Brenden was silent as he strode toward the entrance of the store. Jordan caught up to him, grabbing his hand and dragging him to a stop.

"What did you do?" she asked again, her gold eyes searching his face.

Brenden curled his lips in disgust. "You didn't think I was going to let him stay in your band, did you?"

Jordan's mouth dropped open. "You didn't..."

"I did," Brenden replied, leaning against the wall outside the store and lighting a cigarette.

"Brenden! Now he's going to think I wanted him out," Jordan said, horrified.

"And exactly how were you planning on hiding your pregnancy from him if you had to see him every day on the tour, love?" Brenden asked derisively.

"Didn't you just tell me it was going to become obvious?" Jordan asked. "If you didn't mean the tour, then what?"

"I meant that it'll come out, Jordan." Brenden took a long drag on his cigarette. "You're not exactly an everyday Jane in society. Eventually you'll show, and it'll get photographed. You don't think Dylan's going to figure out that he's the father?"

"He doesn't know that I wasn't sleeping with anyone else."

"Right," Brenden said, rolling his eyes.

"Well, fuck!" she yelled, startling the people walking into the store. "What am I supposed to do, Beege?"

"You need to tell him."

"What good will that do?"

"He needs to know, Jordan," Brenden said. "It's his right."

"You're thinking of you and Allexx, Beege. You two were in love. You had a right to know she was pregnant. Dylan doesn't love me—you pointed that out to me. He's a married man that's never had kids in the eighteen years he's been married. Why tell him now? It's just going to cause problems. What if he wants me to get an abortion? What if he takes me to court? Imagine the press on that."

"Jordie, he can do that either way," Brenden pointed out. "When he figures out that you're pregnant by way of the media. And that might just piss him off enough to sue you."

Jordan shook her head. "Nothing pisses him off, Beege, nothing."

Brenden reached out a finger, sliding it along her jawline affectionately. "You have a singular talent, love, of pissing off saints."

"Thanks!" Jordan exclaimed, making a face.

Brenden grinned, tossing his cigarette down and stepping on it with his booted foot. "You're welcome." He took her hand and headed into the store.

They walked around, picking up the things he needed. Jordan was silent for a while, ignoring the occasional flashes of the ever-present paparazzi cameras. She lived with them daily; she knew no matter what she did, they'd record it.

"You have to undo it, Beege," she told him as they stood in the checkout line.

"Nope," he replied simply, his face set in a serious line.

"Brenden, he's going to think I kicked him out. That's not fair, not after all the hard work he did on the album." Jordan grabbed his arm in her need to convince him.

"He'll get paid for the work he did," Brenden replied coldly.

They were both silent while Brenden paid for his items. He'd added a bottle of Absolut vodka to his purchases. It told Jordan how on edge this conversation was making him. He wanted a drink.

Outside the store, she turned to him. "Brenden, please? I don't want him to hate me."

Brenden stopped walking and looked down at her. "Why does that matter?"

Jordan didn't answer, shaking her head and turning to walk back to the car. Brenden followed. He put the bag in the trunk and got into the car. Jordan was already sitting in the car waiting for him. Brenden turned to her, looking at her for a long time. Eventually he put a finger under her chin and turned her face to his.

"Why does it matter, Jordie?" he asked softly.

She pressed her lips together and shook her head, a sheen of tears in her eyes.

Brenden winced, turning to start the engine of the Lamborghini with a roar. Tires squealed as he backed out of the parking space, and again when he threw it into first gear and roared out of the lot.

It was another few minutes before he calmed down enough to slow down.

"You're in love with him," he said defeatedly.

Jordan didn't say anything. Finally she nodded slowly.

"Goddamn it!" he yelled, slamming his hand on the steering wheel. "Why? Why the fuck do you do this, Jordan?" His tone was pained. "Why do you choose men that are only going to rip your fucking heart out?" He shook his head as if not able to understand, and in truth he couldn't. "You have everything, Jordan. You're beautiful, intelligent, talented as hell. You have money, you have youth, you have everything you've ever wanted. Why the bloody hell can't you find a man that isn't either in love with his ex-wife, related to you, or fucking married?" He yelled the last at the top of his lungs.

Jordan jumped at the sheer volume Brenden hit. There was a reason he was the number-one rock vocalist in the world. He had a range that normal men couldn't reach. That added to his vehemence when he was mad. Then it hit her what he'd just said, and the tears started. She looked out the window, not wanting him to see her crying.

Brenden was immediately sorry he'd said what he had. After a few minutes he blew his breath out, shaking his head.

"I'm sorry, Jord. I just hate to see you get hurt every time." He reached across and took her hand.

Jordan nodded, but she didn't look at him. She hated letting herself fall in love again, knowing it was stupid. She hadn't really realized that she was actually in love with Dylan until she'd known she would lose him. The baby would ruin their relationship, but she wasn't ready to give it up. Of course, running out on him in Vegas probably hadn't helped their relationship at all either. Either way, Jordan knew that she'd never get Dylan full time, and it wasn't her style to be someone's mistress forever. She had needed to choose between the relationship with Dylan, and the baby. And in the end, she decided at least the baby would be with her forever. It didn't make missing Dylan any easier though.

***

Dylan had tried calling Jordan at her house; he'd also tried her cell phone. He got voice mail every time. He didn't leave a message. He didn't like talking to machines. The week before, he'd received a formal letter from Brenden Sparks as CEO of Badlands Records telling him that his contract with Jordan Tate was being terminated. Dylan had read the letter over, his brows furrowing temporarily. Then he'd calmly folded the letter and stuck it in his desk drawer.

Marissa hadn't been so calm when he'd mentioned it to her the following day.

"You've what?"

"Been released," Dylan repeated, leaning back in the chair in his study.

"Why?" she asked, her tone sharp.

"The letter didn't say."

Marissa's eyes narrowed dangerously. "Didn't say?" she repeated sarcastically. "You were fucking Jordan Tate, and now you've fucked your way right out of work, you stupid limey bastard!"

Dylan looked back at her calmly. His face didn't indicated he'd even heard her nasty comments.

"What are you going to do now?" Marissa asked.

Instead of answering, Dylan steepled his fingers and looked at her. "I think I'm going to take a vacation."

"A vacation?" she repeated. "You're going to take a vacation? You're out of work. We're screwed, Dylan, don't you understand that?"

Dylan canted his head to the side. "Now why would you say that?"

Marissa glared at him like he was crazy. "Because, you idiot, we have expenses. You need to find more work."

Dylan looked thoughtful for a moment, then ticked points off on his fingers. "I own my car, we own this house, we have a flat in London that's paid for, I get a monthly check from the royalties of Project that should more than cover household expenses, and I have money in savings. What's the problem?"

Marissa stared back at him open mouthed. She couldn't believe he could be so dumb. Then it occurred to her—he wasn't dumb at all. She pointed an immaculately manicured blood-red fingernail at him.

"If you think for a second that you're done working, Dylan Silver, you can just forget it! I'm not going to stay married to a bum."

Dylan grinned, his eyes more silver than gray.

"Well, that, my love, is the best news I've heard all week."

"What?"

Dylan sat up, placing his hands on the desk in front of him. "I'm divorcing you, Marissa."

"What are you talking about?" She was sure he didn't mean it how he'd just said it.

"I'm talking about a divorce," he replied, still irritatingly calm. "I don't want to be married to you anymore. You've had eighteen years to get everything you can get out of me, and now I'm done giving it to you."

Marissa's face grew nasty as he spoke. "Oh you think so, do you?" she asked snidely. "You've just begun with what you're going to give me, Dylan Silver. You can't divorce me, I won't let you. Do you understand that? Whatever Jordan Tate has put into your head is just bullshit. You won't walk away from me, Dylan. You never have and you never will."

"Don't count on that, Marissa."

"I will!" she screamed, slamming out of the study.

Dylan sat reflecting on the scene. It had gone better than he'd expected it to. Of course, he knew she wasn't done screaming at him. But he fully intended to take the suitcases he had placed in his car and leave that evening. He was checking into a hotel, and he had no intention of dealing with his wife any more than necessary.

Dylan was sitting in his hotel room, typing away on the keyboard of his laptop, when his cell phone rang. He glanced at the display and noted that it said "Caller ID Withheld." He knew it was still likely to be Marissa, using the code to block their number so he wouldn't know it was her. But he answered it anyway, hoping...

"Hello?"

There was a long silence, then her voice. "Dylan, it's Jordan," she said softly. "I need to see you."

"When?" he asked, his voice equally soft. "Where?"

"Can you come to the house?"

"Yes, I can. When do you want me to come?"

"Can you come now?" she asked pleadingly.

"I'll leave now," he said, sensing her turmoil even over the phone line.

A half hour later he knocked on her door. She didn't answer. Finally he tried the door; it was unlocked. He walked inside.

"Jordan?"

"In here," she called from her bedroom.

Dylan walked in and saw her lying on the bed. She didn't look well. What he didn't know was that she'd been throwing up when he rang the doorbell. Her morning sickness hit at odd times of the day. She was lying on the bed in the hopes that she wouldn't get sick again while he was there.

"Are you okay?" he asked, seeing how green she looked.

She nodded, slowly sitting up. "Sit down, please."

He sat down, his hand automatically reaching out to smooth her hair back from her cheek. "I'm glad you called. I needed to talk to you."

"Dylan, let me talk first, please?" Jordan said, wanting to get this over with quickly.

"Okay."

Jordan took a deep breath, suppressing the immediate feeling of nausea.

"I need to tell you something," she began. "But I want you to hear me out before you say anything, okay?"

Dylan nodded.

"First of all, I'm sorry I took off on you in Vegas," she said, looking sincerely so. "Brenden showed up. He was upset about me sleeping with you, and he wanted to take me back to L.A.... Anyway, I'm sorry I left without a word."

Again Dylan nodded, not saying anything, his gray eyes unreadable but his face the picture of calm.

"When I got back here, I hid out at Brenden's house for a while. He's kind of a refuge for me when I need time to think. And I had a lot to think about when I got back from Vegas."

"About Joe?" Dylan asked quietly.

"About you." Jordan's gold eyes searched his face. "About... Well, Brenden had pointed out a few things to me that night. He told me I was crazy for sleeping with you, because you are very, very married."

"Very, very married?" he repeated, slightly amused. "I didn't realize there were levels of married."

Jordan grinned in spite of herself. "Well, you've been married for eighteen years, Dylan, and even though you've had affairs, you've never left her. That would make you very, very married, as in not likely to leave her for the likes of me."

"But—" Dylan began, but her hand on his mouth stopped him.

"Please, let me finish, or I'm not going to be able to," She swallowed convulsively, feeling nauseated again. "Dylan," she said, looking up into his eyes. "I'm pregnant." She kept her hand over his mouth. "And before you say anything, I've decided I want to keep the baby. I won't ask you for anything. I won't even let anyone know you're the father if you want it that way. Brenden said he'd let me put his name on the birth certificate if I wanted him to."

"Always so helpful," Dylan murmured behind her hand.

"What?" Jordan asked, seeing the amused glint in his eyes.

"So you want to keep the baby?" he asked, taking her hand from his mouth and holding it.

"Yes." She didn't understand his mood; he seemed to find this situation funny. "I'll raise it myself. I won't ask you for a thing. I'll even put that in writing."

Dylan nodded. "And what if we raised the child?"

Jordan stared at him, horrified. "You mean you and Marissa?"

"I mean, you and me."

"And Marissa?"

"Jordan," Dylan said, touching her under the chin, his eyes sparkling. "If you'd have let me get a word in edgewise here, I would have told you that I filed for a divorce from Marissa the day I got back from Vegas."

"You what?" Jordan asked, sure she hadn't just heard what he'd said.

"I'm divorcing Marissa."

"Why?" Jordan knew it was a stupid question, but she needed to know.

"Because I'm in love with you," he said, not bothering to play any games.

"You are?" she asked in wonder. This had to be a dream.

"I am," he said, a smile playing at his lips.

"Oh, Dylan…" Jordan said, not sure what to say. "Oh God, all this time… Oh, Dylan… I'm sorry…"

Dylan grinned, leaning in to kiss her lips softly. Jordan wrapped her arms around his neck and kissed him back. He pulled her closer, deepening the kiss. As he made love to her, Jordan was extremely thankful to realize her nausea had abated. Dylan reminded her over and over again why she'd missed his body so much.

Afterwards, curled up in his arms, she looked up at him.

"I love you," she said, her gold eyes shining brightly in the dying light of the sun.

He kissed her, then pulled back to look at her. "When my divorce is final, will you marry me?"

Jordan bit her lip, thrilled beyond belief at what he'd just said. "Yes, oh my God, yes," she said, nodding vehemently.

He hugged her to him, kissing her temple and holding her close. He knew this was right. It felt so good being with her, and he'd missed her more than he'd ever missed anything in his life. Even his music didn't fill the void now—only she could do that. That's how he knew he belonged with her.

"Were you ever going to call me?" she asked later that evening while he cooked in her kitchen.

"Yes," Dylan assured her. "I was going to wait to be further into divorce proceedings, but I wasn't letting you go that easily."

Jordan smiled, happy to know that it hadn't been the fact that she was pregnant that made him want her. But then again that was obvious. He'd filed for divorce even after she'd left him high and dry in Vegas. She shook her head again as she realized what an incredible man he was.

"What?" he asked, catching the shake of her head.

"I was just thinking about what a fantastic man you are," she said, reaching out to touch his cheek from where she sat on the counter. "I mean, so many men would have been so pissed off that I'd left like that. They would have held a grudge or something, but not you..."

Dylan shrugged. "I figured you had your reasons. Obviously, I wasn't happy about it, but being angry over something I didn't understand wasn't going to solve anything."

Jordan was amazed by him. "Do you think if I'm married to you long enough, I'll learn to be like you?"

"Like me?" he asked with a grin.

"Yeah, you know, so centered and logical about things."

Dylan put down the knife he was cutting vegetables with and stood in front of her. He put his arms around her and kissed her lips.

"You are who you are, Jordan, and I love you."

"Yes, but I don't want to be like Marissa is to you. I don't want to be the drama queen that I've been before..."

Dylan's finger stilled her head, his eyes looking into hers.

"Jordan, I'm not Joe," he said without a trace of anger in his voice. "You don't scare me with your temper or your bad moods or your so-called drama. You're not going to run me off. Haven't you seen that already?"

Jordan realized that she had. She had been sure this last stunt would have done it, but it didn't. He came right back when she called. He let her have her way, but not to the point of walking on him.

"You are the calm to my storm," she said, having thought that before about his unperturbable way.

Dylan grinned. "An excellent lyric if I ever heard one."

Jordan laughed. "True, too bad we're already done with the album."

"Has it been cut?"

"No," she said. "Beege hasn't green-lighted it yet. He's still 'living' with it."

Living with it was something Brenden did with all the albums that came out of his recording studios. Every album that was made in his studios to be released by Badlands had to go through Brenden. He had final say on whether or not it was released. He'd killed entire albums before because he felt the music wasn't up to par. So Brenden would get a CD burned ahead of time so he could listen to it over and over again and "live with it" for a while, deciding if he liked it or not. Deciding if he wanted more added, or edits made. He had final creative control on all albums. It was written into every contract any band signed with his company, no matter who they were. Jordan was included in that.

Dylan nodded, knowing exactly how Brenden operated. "Has he said anything about it yet?"

Jordan smiled. "He's told me that if this is what comes out of having really good sex while writing, he'll hire me someone for every album. Does that count?"

Dylan laughed at that. "Well, hopefully he'll be relieved to hear that he won't need to hire anyone, right?"

Jordan smiled, still unable to believe that this was really happening. "I think if he's not happy for me, I'll beat him over the head until he is."

Dylan grinned. He understood Brenden's attitude. Dylan was a married man, and getting involved with Jordan had created a problem. Brenden had been in the business long enough to know

91

all about Dylan's affairs. Insiders in the entertainment industry knew about them; in fact, many of his friends in the industry had helped cover a number of the affairs. They'd all understood that Marissa was a shrew, and although no one had ever understood why Dylan wouldn't leave his wife, they liked him enough to help keep him out of trouble with her.

So Brenden would have assumed that Jordan was just another affair to Dylan. And she would have been, but she'd shown him something he hadn't encountered before. She had an underlying vulnerability that he'd seen, and she responded to his gentle assurance. He felt like she needed him, and that felt good. He'd had a woman relying on him financially for years—for that reason he'd sought out women who needed nothing from him in that area. Jordan had been the same. But she'd come to need him for something he was desperate to give to someone, emotional support. She needed his love, his understanding, his caring, and his calm. He truly was the calm to her storm, and that made him feel whole. She was what he needed.

***

The following day, Jordan and Dylan slept in, having been up half the night making love and enjoying each other. They woke early in the afternoon. Dylan made them omelets, and they sat on her balcony overlooking the pool, eating and drinking coffee. Brenden came by to check on Jordan, to assure himself that she was okay. He entered her house, noticing the gold Jaguar out front. He suspected it was Dylan's but wanted to make sure.

He heard them talking out on the balcony and walked out there.

"Good morning," he said. Jordan was in her robe, and Dylan wore only pants.

"Beege!" Smiling brightly, Jordan got up to hug him.

Brenden hugged her, his focus on Dylan. The other man looked back at him, his eyes silver in the sunlight. Dylan didn't look away, and Brenden's eyes narrowed slightly.

"So..." Brenden said, sitting down and picking up Jordan's coffee. He took a sip, his eyes on Dylan again. "What did I miss?"

Brenden was always direct, rarely playing games when someone he cared about was involved.

"BJ!" Jordan exclaimed, not wanting him to intimidate Dylan. She didn't realize that nothing intimidated Dylan.

Dylan took her hand and pulled her down onto his lap, looking directly back at Brenden. "I'm divorcing Marissa, Jordan and I are getting married, and she's having our child," he recited calmly.

Brenden's mouth dropped open in shock, then it was obvious his cynical mind took over.

"And when are you actually divorcing Marissa?" he asked with disbelief.

"I filed two and a half weeks ago," Dylan replied, still calm even in the face of Brenden's obvious accusation.

"You did?" Brenden asked, once again stunned.

Dylan nodded. Jordan glanced down at Dylan, worried that Brenden was offending him. She saw that he was grinning. She looked back at Brenden; he was nodding now too.

"I misjudged you." Brenden's voice showed his surprise at having been wrong.

"I'm sure it won't be the last time," Dylan said, his grin in place.

Brenden laughed.

***

Things moved quickly. Brenden set the release of Jordan's third album, aptly entitled *Through The Storm*, for two months from then. The tour was set to start two weeks after the release, and even that was hastily planned. Brenden had a team of four people working to set up tour dates and all arrangements. His daughter Tabitha was one of the team.

Tabitha, who'd known Jordan for years and looked at her as the older sister she'd never had, was thrilled to hear that Jordan was not only pregnant but getting married too. Tabitha knew about Joe Sinclair—had, in fact, met him during the tour he'd accompanied them on for a bit. Tabitha also knew that it had hurt Jordan a great deal when Joe had broken it off with her.

The critics were already hailing the album as the coming-of-age album for Jordan Tate, with quotes such as "Songs that grab you and won't let go from start to finish" and "Jordan Tate has reached inside and shown us everything." Fans were clamoring for the release of the album. Being the spin master that he was, Brenden had released snippets of the first single on Jordan's website. People were excited.

So was Jordan. She knew this was her best work yet, and she knew it had everything to do with Dylan's lyrics. Every chance she got, she credited him with writing the songs.

Their relationship was, however, kept quiet, as was Jordan's condition. Only key, trusted people at Badlands even knew she was pregnant. It was something Brenden had discussed with them. Dylan was willing to go along with whatever Jordan wanted. Jordan was swayed by Brenden telling her that Dylan's divorce, already becoming a nightmare, would go more smoothly if Marissa didn't know about the baby. So Dylan and Jordan did their best not to show too much affection when they were in public together. They were, however, seen together quite often. Jordan refused to totally hide out; she wanted to be with him all the time.

In private, they were together constantly. They spent all their time talking, making love, or cooking in her kitchen. Jordan found that more and more Dylan was the man who was meant for her. He was able to talk to her about anything and everything, like

Joe had been able to, but with one major difference. Dylan was a musician, and he'd also had his time with doing drugs and drinking. He understood what she'd been through, and he didn't look down on her for that. He also understood music industry people, how they acted, why they did what they did, and that meant he understood her.

She reveled in Dylan's tenderness, but also thoroughly enjoyed their lovemaking. He was forever coming up with new ways to excite her, yet he always remained the loving, caring man he was. She spent so many nights in his arms, hoping nothing would happen to ruin what they had. The relationship with Joe had shown her that no matter what she thought, things could always be ruined. Her biggest concern was Dylan's divorce.

Marissa Silver was not going quietly. She was fighting every aspect of the divorce, countering everything Dylan put in writing. He would get countless messages daily from her, screaming at him, telling him she'd take everything he had if he didn't wise up and come home. Marissa was not fooled by their low profile in the press—she knew he was staying with Jordan, and it infuriated her no end. No woman had ever taken Dylan away from her. Jordan Tate wouldn't be the first.

***

When the tour began two and a half months later, Jordan was four and a half months pregnant. She'd had her costumes designed to hide her pregnancy when she began to show. Even so, the tour was purposely kept short, only three months, hitting the major cities. Brenden apologized to the entire band for putting them on such a tight tour schedule, but he wanted to make sure the album sold as it should, while also protecting their "little family secret," as they'd started calling Jordan's pregnancy. The entire band was behind Dylan and Jordan's union; they'd seen first hand the effect

Dylan had on her. They all agreed to the strenuous schedule for that reason.

They all flew, on the Badlands jet, to the first show destination, in Tallahassee, Florida. The buses would meet them there, and the traveling would start. There was a show almost every day, with a few one- or two-day breaks in between. When they arrived at the stadium the show was in, Jordan went about getting her sound check done, while Dylan and the rest of the band tuned up and did their sound checks as well. Jordan waited at the side of the stage, watching Dylan. She watched him interact with the other members of the band and the road crew. He had an easygoing, open personality that made people like him immediately. He joked with the crew and band members, talking about the latest stats on how the England soccer team was doing in the World Cup.

She was ever amazed by him, and she loved that he was such an open person. Dylan related better to her band than even she did. She'd always avoided getting too close to her band members for the very reason that her bassist had ended up quitting. Because they all thought they could get into her pants. She didn't trust them. She didn't trust men in general.

In her lifetime, she'd made the mistake of trusting a few men. First Mark, her stepbrother. His mother had married her father. Mark had set out to conquer her and had. When she'd tried to break off the relationship, he became violent, beating her. Then when she'd made it, he'd decided to become her manager. He threatened, terrified, and hurt her for years after that. It had been Joe who'd rescued her from Mark, literally buying him out of his contract with her to the tune of $750,000.

Then there'd been Jim, the bodyguard hired by Brenden to protect her from Mark if he ever tried to come after her. She hadn't totally trusted Jim; he'd come on to her too many times for that. But in Las Vegas the year before, he'd attacked her. Joe had been the one to fly to be by her side then too. He'd ended up staying on as her personal security until the end of the tour. It was no wonder Joe had become such an icon of the perfect man to her. He'd rescued her so often in such a short period of time. Being right where she needed him when she needed him most. He was a hard act to follow, but Dylan had her heart now, and she was glad in so many ways that he did.

Jordan did have to admit she was developing a lot of affection for her bandmates now, however. They'd stood by her during this change in her life. They were very supportive of her relationship with Dylan, telling her they thought he was good for her. It made her feel good.

***

The very first show made it obvious that Jordan Tate had changed. She wore an outfit that wasn't as outrageously sexy as the ones she'd worn before, but it was still very much her— a long sweeping jacket, form-fitting butter-soft leather pants, and a long gold silk shirt over a black silk-and-lace camisole. Her boots had only two-inch heels, with laces up the side to her knees. She was still incredibly beautiful, and very sexy regardless of the lack of skin showing. Her show, as always, wowed them. Her voice had grown, with the help of Brenden's coaching, and Dylan's songs that stretched her range.

She also had a habit of winking at her new bassist and smiling brightly. Something that was not lost on the fans. Jordan Tate and Dylan Silver were both credited with the writing of the album, although Jordan gave Dylan all of the credit. They'd been seen together often enough to make people wonder if a love affair was going on. Dylan was no longer wearing the wedding band he'd always worn, and that was not lost on the press. Brenden had no comment to make when he was contacted about Dylan Silver's marital status. Dylan's agent also had no comment, per

Dylan's instructions. No sense in inciting Marissa by releasing the news that they were divorcing.

The first show went well, and Jordan did three encores, thrilling the crowd. The last encore was a song she did in an acoustic set, with only piano behind her, which Dylan played. The song was a duet. She'd managed to convince Dylan to sing with her. Even though he'd claimed he couldn't sing, he could indeed, and beautifully so. The song they sang together was the one they'd written at the last minute to add to the album before its release, "Calm The Storm." The lyrics talked about being in the storm of life, when everything goes wrong and you can't control it. When the seas tossed you another crashing disappointment and you had to go on somehow. The chorus—"I turn to you, my safe haven, battle weary and worn, and you are the calm to my storm"—was them, so it was easy for them to sing it like they meant it, because they did.

It was also easy enough for her to be able to flirt with him when he was the only band member on stage. She walked behind him, trailing her hand over his shoulders. Leaning down, she whispered in his ear, kissing it before she moved away. Dylan grinned, shaking his head at her. She was enjoying herself, he could see that, and he was enjoying watching her in action. It thrilled him no end to hear his lyrics sung with her incredible voice and to be able to share this with her. He knew they were right together.

The crowd loved the song, screaming and cheering long after Jordan and Dylan took their final bows and brought the other band members out to bow again too. Even after the lights came up, people were still cheering. Dylan and Jordan were elated; their album was going to be a hit.

That night in the hotel room, they made love basking in the thrill of knowing that what they'd created together was going to be well received. They lay together afterwards, their bodies intertwined.

"Promise me that we'll always have this," she said wistfully, smiling at him.

"We will." Dylan kissed her. "We have a common ground a lot of people don't share."

"Music," she said.

"Yes," he replied. "And a desire to see it done the best it can be."

"I'm not the perfectionist that you and Beege are though."

"No," Dylan said. "But then that wouldn't work if you were, because one person's version of perfect is only their point of view. What you do have, love, is an intrinsic desire to make something you're proud of, and that's where BJ and I can help you."

"Where you two already have, you mean."

"Indeed," he said, smiling.

***

As the tour continued, the album sales skyrocketed, shooting past Jordan's previous sales. She'd tapped a new market. People that had written her off as some flash in the pan, or just another sex kitten with no real talent, were hearing the first single off the album, and it was good. The lyrics weren't simple bubblegum—they had deeper meanings, ones that hit home. Jordan's voice and those lyrics blended to be both haunting and mesmerizing.

Unfortunately, as the tour wore on, it started to wear Jordan down. Being onstage almost every night, singing her heart out, was taking its toll on her energy and her voice. Three weeks into the tour, her voice was getting ragged. Dylan mobilized immediately, getting her tea and making her rest more. At night when they got to the hotel, he made sure she had a hot bath, keeping her good and warm afterwards with a bathrobe and keeping the room heated. He had the tour manager buy a humidifier for the room to keep her throat moist throughout the night. He also called Brenden to have her appearances curtailed so she would have to talk as little as possible during the day.

Jordan did whatever Dylan suggested, letting him take care of her. It felt good to have him there. He had so much more experience in the music field; he knew all the tricks and what to do for her. Brenden and Dylan had almost daily conversations about how Jordan was doing. They'd actually become friends over the last few months. Dylan had always respected Brenden's work, knowing that Brenden was a very talented and dedicated artist, like himself. Brenden too had respected Dylan for a long time. They'd also found a common interest in seeing that Jordan was not only taken care of, but as happy as humanly possible. Dylan made her happy. That made Brenden like him even more.

When they had a two-day break, thankfully shortly after Jordan's voice started failing, Dylan disappeared for a few hours. He'd left Jordan sleeping in their hotel suite. When she woke, she walked into the kitchen area of the suite to find Dylan cooking. Vegetables were laid out before him, a pan boiling away on the small stove. He was cutting up meat to add to the soup he was making.

"Where did all this come from?" she asked, gesturing to all he had around him.

Dylan grinned. "I made some connections downstairs in the kitchen," he said, winking at her.

"Ahh," she said, smiling. "And you're making me soup?"

"Yes," he said. "Something to help your throat."

"Mmm…" She sniffed the steam coming up from the boiling pot. "Smells really good." Then she smelled something else. Glancing around, she spotted a bread machine on the counter. "Bread too?"

"Mm-hmm. Thought you could use some good healthy food for a change."

Jordan walked over to him, wrapping her arms around his waist from behind and hugging him. "You take good care of me. Thank you."

"Well, I have an ulterior motive." He turned around and kissed her softly.

"And what's that?"

Without a word, he put his hand on her slightly rounded abdomen, staring into her eyes.

"Ahh, so you're taking care of me and our baby," she said, smiling fondly.

"Oh yes." He smiled.

"I think I can live with that," she said, putting her arms around his neck.

He pulled her to him and kissed her, his hands caressing her back.

"I love you," she said against his lips.

"And I love you."

That evening they had dinner in their room, enjoying the sunset and drinking wine. Afterwards they sat on the couch, watching TV, with Jordan curling up in Dylan's arms. It was a relaxing two days, and it put them back on track for the tour.

A week later, Jordan's temper got the better of her when one of the venue managers gave her a dressing room the size of a closet. She screamed at the man for ten minutes. She reminded him that Badlands Records used his venue for a lot of shows. She also told him that if she didn't get a decent dressing room she was going to contact the CEO himself, her personal friend, BJ Sparks.

The manager wrung his hands. "But Ms. Tate, I'm sorry, the rooms are under construction. I tried to tell them when they called to set things up…"

"Who did you talk to?" Jordan asked imperiously.

"I don't know…" the man stammered.

"You better figure it out."

Dylan walked up. He'd been retrieved by one of the road crew.

"Jordan," he said, his voice the epitome of calm. "I'm sure we can work this out, love. Just give the man a chance..."

The venue manager looked relieved that someone had arrived who apparently wasn't going to yell at him.

"Dylan, my dressing room is smaller than the damned bathroom on the bus!" Jordan snapped.

Dylan looked at the manager.

"It's the only thing we have," the manager said plaintively.

"How far is the nearest decent hotel from here?" Dylan asked, his hand on Jordan's arm to silence her.

"There's a Sheraton a mile away," the manager offered hopefully.

Dylan nodded. "Can I ask you to book Jordan a suite there right away?"

"Dylan..." Jordan began, irritated that this was having to take place.

"It's alright, love," he said softly.

Jordan quieted, but not before giving both the venue manager and Dylan a scathing look as she stormed away.

At the hotel, she snapped at Dylan the second they walked in the door.

"Thanks for taking that right out of my hands," she said, her tone anything but grateful. "I felt like an idiot standing there."

Dylan walked over to the couch and sat down. "I thought this might be more comfortable for you than a dressing room."

"That isn't the point!" she snapped.

Dylan considered for a moment, then nodded. "I'm sorry. I didn't mean to usurp you."

Jordan stared at him, then took a minute to look around the suite she'd been booked, courtesy of the venue manager. It occurred to her that she was being a bitch. She dropped her head, walking over to kneel in front of where he sat on the couch.

"No, I'm sorry," she said, looking up into his eyes. "I'm being unreasonable. I'm sorry." Her face reflected worry and sudden terror, and Dylan knew immediately what she was thinking.

He touched her cheek, his eyes looking down into hers. Taking her hand, he pulled her up and onto his lap. He cuddled her close, kissing her forehead.

"Not going to run me off, love. Remember that," he said softly.

She relaxed against him, sighing. "I am sorry, Dylan. You were right. This is much nicer."

It was yet another disaster averted. Jordan quickly found that he wouldn't argue with her. He also never shut her out. But at one point midway through the tour, she also found out that he wouldn't take any and all abuse from her.

When they arrived in Chicago, they were all tired, having just come off a seven-day stretch of shows every night. There had been a malfunction with the air conditioning, so the bus was extremely hot. Jordan was feeling the effects of not only the heat but exhaustion as well. Her hormones were still in an uproar, adjusting to the third trimester of her pregnancy. When they reached the hotel, three hours later than expected due to traffic, and were told by a less than helpful redheaded young woman that the hotel had no record of a reservation for them, Jordan lost it.

"You better fucking *find* the reservation!" she screamed.

"Jordan, just wait..." Dylan cautioned softly behind her.

"No, goddamn it, no!" She turned to him, her eyes blazing. "I'm sick to fucking death of people being ridiculously inept!"

"Give them a chance to find the reservation, love," Dylan said. "Ma'am, can you check under Badlands? Perhaps the reservation was booked under that."

"Just stay out of it, Dylan!" Jordan said, mad that he was going around her again. "I can handle this, you know. I've been doing it for a long time."

Dylan looked back at her for a moment. "Alright," he said, stepping back.

The redhead complained the entire time she looked for the reservation, muttering about rock stars and their egos. Jordan got madder and madder. When there was no reservation to be found, and then they were told that there were no rooms available, Jordan had a fit. Dylan calmly suggested that they contact another hotel for a reservation.

"I'm not traveling all over Bumfuck, Egypt, today, Dylan," she snapped at him. "I'm hot and tired, and they need to give us a room, dammit—they lost the reservation. And I'm not leaving until they accommodate us."

Again Dylan looked back at her, his gray eyes unreadable. Stepping around Jordan, he moved toward the poor young woman that had just witnessed Jordan's barrage. She looked terrified that Dylan was going to start in on her.

"Would you be so kind as to hand me a phone book?"

The young woman looked surprised, but she nodded, rushing to comply. She handed him the book.

"Thank you, love," he said, smiling at the woman.

He proceeded to turn on his heel and walk over to the couches in the lobby of the hotel. Sitting down and pulling out his cell phone, he started making phone calls. Jordan watched in open-mouthed silence, shooting the young woman behind the counter a vile look. The manager came up at that point, and Jordan engaged in a heated discussion with him about the lost reservation. He made the mistake of suggesting that perhaps the error was made by the Badlands staff. Jordan went off on him.

"We're not leaving here, so you'd better find us rooms," she said, crossing her arms in front of her chest.

Dylan walked up, handed the phone book back to the young woman, and thanked her again. Moving to stand behind Jordan, he lowered his head to talk to her.

"While you're standing here making your point," he said evenly, "we'll be headed two miles down the street to a hotel that actually *has* rooms. When you've finished making your point, call me. I'll send the bus back for you."

With that he walked away. Jordan was stunned. She was further shocked that the rest of the band followed Dylan out of the hotel and climbed back onto the bus. She stood staring as the bus drove off. Jordan couldn't believe it. He'd left her there.

She stood in the lobby for another half hour, knowing she looked like a fool. As she moved to the couch, tears of frustration started. The woman had been mean and insulting, and she just got so mad... She hadn't meant to be nasty to Dylan. When her temper was roused, she turned it on anyone that got in the way, and Dylan was always insinuating himself between her and whoever she was mad at. But he'd just shut her down completely, without raising his voice, without threatening, and without causing a scene.

Jordan called Dylan's cell phone, afraid of the reception she'd get when he answered the phone.

"Hello?"

"Dylan, it's me," she said softly.

"The bus'll be outside in three minutes, babe," he replied, his voice equally soft.

"Okay," she said, sounding quite repentant.

She hung up before she made a bigger fool out of herself by begging him to forgive her in front of everyone in the lobby.

The bus arrived. She got on and rode the quick trip to the next hotel. When she got up to the room Dylan had reserved for them, he opened the door. She stood in the doorway, her face drawn and worried. Dylan opened his arms, and she walked into them. He held her close, kicking the door closed with his foot. She found that he'd already ordered them dinner and had a bottle of water waiting for her. He said nothing about her tantrum at the other hotel. He knew he'd made his point.

Jordan learned quickly not to turn her venom on him, because he wouldn't just take it. Usually she was in the wrong, it was just her temper, and he wouldn't be walked on just because she was having a bad day. It was one thing to be mild mannered, another thing to take unnecessary abuse. He'd done that too long; he wouldn't do it with Jordan too. He'd just handle things his way. And Jordan came to appreciate his way.

The rest of the tour proceeded uneventfully. Jordan and Dylan grew closer and closer emotionally. Jordan knew he was her soulmate. They had everything in common. Even their experiences and excesses with drugs and alcohol. Dylan had gone through a phase of booze and drugs years before, but had cleaned up when he'd seen his health taking a turn for the worse. He refused to become a stereotypical rock star. Jordan found it quite comforting that he'd done drugs too. Unlike with Joe. She'd always felt like a miscreant with Joe, because he'd been so clean.

Joe had never really condemned her for her use, but he'd been quite succinct about telling her she couldn't use and be with him at the same time. Dylan didn't have such an edict, but Jordan also didn't fight with Dylan like she'd fought with Joe, so she had less need to use. She found she never craved the drugs she'd used for years. Dylan was enough of a high for her.

They made their way from one end of the country to the other, spending all their time together when they weren't performing. Jordan found that one of her other fears about Dylan had been groundless. She'd been concerned that he was too frugal for her, would think she was a horrible person for spending what she did on clothes and shoes. He'd made a few comments in the beginning of their relationship about Marissa's habit of buying everything under the sun whether she needed it or not. So Jordan had worried that this would be an issue for them. She found out that Dylan had absolutely no problem with her spending habits. When she questioned him about it, referring to the comments he'd made about Marissa's thinking money grew on trees, his response was simply "Marissa was spending my hard-earned money. You're spending yours."

"So, will it be different when we're married?" Jordan asked.

Dylan shrugged. "I imagine you'll always make more than me, since you're the star, so I can't foresee it being any of my business." When he could see she was still concerned, he continued. "Jordan, Marissa never contributed to the marriage financially, unless you count running up the bills. But she had no problem spending like she made at least half. We're not in that situation. I'm not difficult about money—I just like to feel like my partner is giving as well as taking."

Jordan nodded. "So since I'm bringing my own bank account to the marriage, it's okay, right?"

"Right." Dylan grinned. "Besides, you don't seem to have to have a new fur coat to go with every outfit…"

"I don't wear fur," Jordan said, making a face.

"Good. You wouldn't be who I thought you were if you did."

Jordan smiled at that. They'd already talked about their feelings on just about every issue in the world, one of which was the issue of furs and animals, et cetera. She'd found that as with everything else, Dylan always had intelligent, educated opinions. She loved that about him. It felt good to be around him. He was intelligent, but never condescending about it.

***

Before they knew it, the last show was upon them. As usual, they saved the duet for last. The duet between Jordan and Dylan had been getting a great deal of press. The reason for that was that the last one Jordan had done was with Brenden, and it was written by Brenden when they were a couple. The new duet, written by Dylan Silver and Jordan Tate, made people wonder if something was indeed going on between Jordan and her new bassist.

As always, Jordan was totally in tune with the song. It thrilled her no end that it was truly how she and Dylan felt about each other, so she really let herself go when they sang it. On this night, their last show, she gave up being cautious, because it was so hot in the stadium. She threw off her jacket, tossing it up on the piano as she sang. It was very obvious to anyone paying attention that there was a very definite bulge to her middle.

She was six and a half months pregnant and was showing, although not greatly, simply a rounding of her belly. It was enough to cause a huge stir in the entertainment industry. If the rumors were true and she was dating her bassist, Dylan Silver was a married man. The questions of "Is Jordan Tate home-wrecking again?" started almost immediately. They were the same questions the press asked when Jordan had been dating Joe, thinking that Jordan had been the reason for Joe's divorce.

Jordan and Dylan managed to escape the press that night, but soon the news was everywhere. Their secret was more or less out, although neither Jordan nor Dylan, nor Badlands Records, had any comment on the matter.

**

The morning she read the paper, Marissa Silver threw a screaming fit the likes of which had never before been witnessed in Starbucks. The not-so-subtle "Is Jordan Tate carrying Dylan Silver's first child?" hit her like a ton of bricks. Marissa couldn't believe it. He wouldn't dare! He wouldn't get her pregnant! She didn't care if they were supposed to be getting a divorce—Marissa had never honestly believed that Dylan would go through with it. But he'd gotten Jordan Tate pregnant? No, that couldn't be true. She must have gotten pregnant by one of the hundreds of men she slept with. No, Dylan wouldn't do this to her, no... Maybe Jordan was trying to pin it on him. Dylan could be very naive; maybe he had no idea. That was it—he was trying to be gallant. Damned Englishmen!

Marissa calmed herself. Finally she had a way to keep Dylan and get rid of that Tate bitch once and for all. Jordan Tate would never have him; Marissa would see to that no matter what it took. She thanked the young woman who handed her the latte she'd ordered and walked out. She didn't notice that every person in the place was staring at her like she was crazy.

***

Dylan was surprised when he got a call from Marissa. He wasn't surprised because she'd called; he'd expected that. What surprised him was that she sounded totally reasonable on the phone.

"Dylan, can we meet to talk?" Marissa asked sweetly.

"Talk about what?" His voice didn't reflect his surprise in the least.

"I'd like to work things out."

Dylan was silent a moment, then finally said, "Alright, meet me in half an hour at the pier."

"I'll be there," Marissa said, her tone a little on the playful side.

Dylan hung up without a response.

Jordan was out buying groceries. Dylan wrote a quick note, left it on the refrigerator, and picked up his keys.

Dylan leaned against the front fender of his car, his ankles crossed, his hands on either side of him on the hood. He wore white cotton drawstring pants, a tan short-sleeved shirt, and tan deck shoes. With his sunglasses covering his eyes and his dark hair blowing in the ocean breeze, he was the picture of California casual. Marissa had to admit he was still a handsome man. Even his eyes were such an interesting color, gray shot through with silver, not that she could see them now with his glasses on.

Walking up, she looked him over. He looked healthy, and disturbingly happy. She saw that he'd had the damage she'd caused to his beloved gold Jaguar repaired as well. It had served him right, being such an asshole when he'd left town with that slut. He'd left her with his car; she'd just had a few "accidents" with it. Of course he'd had the car repaired—it was one of the most important things he owned. Perhaps it was even a surrogate for the baby they'd never had.

Marissa reached up to kiss him. Dylan pulled his head back, jerking it away from her. Marissa narrowed her eyes at him but said nothing. No sense in starting off fighting.

"You wanted to talk?" Dylan said amicably.

"Yes," Marissa said, leaning against his car next to him. "I was hoping we could work some things out."

"For instance?" he asked.

Marissa glanced over at him, her smile sweet. "Well, I was thinking that we could try for a baby again."

Dylan's eyebrows furrowed, as he was literally stunned into silence. He opened his mouth not once but twice to say something, and then closed it again. He wasn't sure where he'd missed something, but he apparently had.

"A baby?" he finally managed, his tone every bit as puzzled as he was.

"Yes." Marissa sounded upbeat; she'd obviously mistaken his confusion. "I know I said that I didn't want to try again, but I think it would really help bring us closer together. You know?" She peered up at him, her brown eyes searching his face.

Dylan turned and reached into his car for a cigarette, feeling the need to do something, anything, to avoid this conversation. Was she nuts? Did she really think that bringing a child into the ruins of their marriage would fix it? Then it hit him: she knew about Jordan and thought that was why he was divorcing her for Jordan. A baby? Is that all she thought it was about? She was indeed crazy. No, he corrected himself—she was, as always, so self-involved she had no idea that he'd never been truly happy in their marriage. She figured it had to be something he was lacking that she could just hand him. What he'd been lacking was love, and Marissa had no clue what that was, so she couldn't give it to him.

The problem was, he had no idea how to get around this one without causing a huge fight. Taking a deep breath, he plunged in anyway.

"Marissa," he began calmly, "our marriage is far beyond a simple fix. I was hoping we could come to some kind of agreement on the divorce."

Marissa stared back at him, her face reflecting shock that he hadn't jumped at her offer. Then it changed, and Dylan could see the venom fill her.

"Oh, that's not going to happen, Dylan. You're not going to be able to marry your pregnant slut, so forget it," she spat. "Do you think I'm a complete fool? Do you think I'll just let our marriage go like that? No, I won't, so you'd better wise up and come back home with me now."

Dylan shook his head. How did one reason with totally illogical thinking? Marissa thought that just because she didn't want to let him go, that he couldn't go?

"She'll never have you, Dylan!" Marissa screeched. "You're mine, you always have been. You've never left me for anyone, and you're not going to start now. Do you understand that?"

Dylan looked back at her, his eyes full of pity, not alarm. Well, he should be alarmed, she thought.

"I'll kill you before she has you, Dylan Scott Silver. You'd better know that," she growled.

Dylan lifted his chin, his face closing off. She'd just triggered his shutdown button. When she started making threats, he stopped listening, because he knew it signaled an end to her sense of any reason, and he didn't have the energy to listen to any more of it today. Straightening, he tossed away his cigarette, blowing the smoke out in a long stream.

"It's been lovely," he said politely, and got into his car.

Marissa stepped back, surprised. She looked pensive even as he started the Jaguar with a low rumble. As he put the car into reverse, she reached into her pocket, pulled out a cell phone, and started dialing a number. Dylan didn't stick around to watch. He drove out of the parking lot and headed back toward Jordan's house in Malibu.

It was almost dark and Dylan wanted to get back, knowing Jordan would be worried that he went to talk to Marissa. Jordan didn't trust Marissa as far as she could throw her. Perhaps even less than that.

Dylan had just rounded a corner on the highway when headlights behind him came dangerously close to hitting him. He glanced in his rearview mirror. It was a good thing the guy hadn't hit him. The vehicle behind him was a big truck, not something Dylan wanted to tangle with on a two-lane highway a mile above the ocean with nothing but a drop-off to the left and a cliff face to the right.

Dylan sped up a bit as he noticed that the guy was now tailgating him.

"Lovely," he muttered.

He waited for an opportunity then pulled to the right to let the driver of the truck pass. The truck didn't pass him. He swerved to the right as well and clipped Dylan's bumper.

"Bloody hell..." Dylan exclaimed as he grappled to get the steering wheel under control. The Jaguar swerved dangerously into the oncoming lane as Dylan corrected his headlong plunge toward the drop-off. Dylan pulled it back into the correct lane, glancing behind him. He expected to see the truck pulling off to deal with the possible accident he could have just caused. Instead the truck was right on his tail again.

"What the..." Dylan began to say out loud just as the truck sped up and slammed into him from behind once more.

Again Dylan fought the steering wheel, using every ounce of concentration to keep the car from heading over the edge of the nearby cliff. There was no time to think, no time to wonder why the guy was trying to kill him. Dylan had time to react, nothing more. It became very obvious very quickly that the driver of the truck was intent on putting him over the cliff. Dylan made a split-second decision, praying it was the right thing to do.

The driver of the truck was shocked, although not totally displeased, when the gold Jaguar veered to actually slam into the cliff face. The dark-haired man in the truck grinned to himself as he kept driving. Mission accomplished.

♫ FOUR ♫

Brenden drove an almost hysterical Jordan to the hospital. They'd been told the bare minimum. Dylan Silver had been involved in a car accident on the highway; he was being Life-Flighted to Cedars-Sinai. Nothing more.

"Life Flight?" Jordan queried, her hands clenched together in her lap. "That means he was hurt badly, doesn't it?"

Brenden glanced over at her, then back at the road. "Doesn't necessarily mean that, Jordie. Palisades is a more remote road—maybe they figured the helo was faster. Don't panic yet, okay? Let's just get there and see how he is."

Jordan nodded, feeling absolutely sick. The baby was doing somersaults in her belly, sensing Jordan's tension and worry. She ran her hands over her tummy, trying to soothe both herself and the baby inside. The drive to the hospital took far too long, but Jordan kept herself calm. She knew that getting too upset could cause her to go into early labor, and the last thing she wanted was to lose this baby. If she lost Dylan though… Her mind reeled at the thought. No, she couldn't lose him, she couldn't… not now…

Brenden took charge as he always did wherever he was. Striding into the hospital, Jordan's hand clenched in his, he walked right up to the admitting nurse.

"I need information on Dylan Silver."

"Are you family?" the nurse asked automatically.

"Yeah," Brenden said, without missing a beat.

The nurse peered at him, recognizing his face but not sure from where. Even so, she looked up the information on Dylan Silver.

"He's in surgery now. The doctor should be out soon," she said efficiently. "Have a seat."

Brenden rolled his eyes. These people needed to get new lines. He turned to Jordan to see that she was gasping for breath.

"Slow down, babe." He put his arm around her and guided her toward the couch in the waiting room. "Hold on to me. It's okay, slow down, Jordie... Come on..." His tone was soothing, his hand rubbing her back gently.

She nodded and did her best to slow her breathing. The baby was kicking hard in response to Jordan's upset. Brenden glanced down and saw the movement of Jordan's belly. He grinned.

"Soccer player for sure, huh?"

"Or a goddamned Rockette," Jordan gasped.

Jordan and Brenden waited in the waiting room, even as the paparazzi arrived to take pictures. Brenden scowled at them but did nothing, knowing that anything he did would only incite them further.

Tabitha and Allexxiss arrived a little while after they got there. Tabitha hugged Jordan, while Allexxiss went to Brenden's side. She and Jordan had come to a truce a while before when Brenden and Allexxiss had gotten together. Jordan had seen Allexxiss hurt Brenden once too often and hadn't liked her because of it. When it was obvious to Jordan that Brenden was very much in love with his wife, however, Jordan couldn't help but give in. Brenden was her best friend, after all.

A few more minutes later, the doctor came out to talk to them. He was a short, thin man with a brown mustache and kind brown eyes. Jordan noticed his eyes, because they were trained on her. Was it in sympathy?

"Are you Ms. Tate?" the doctor surprised her by asking.

Jordan nodded, thinking maybe he just recognized her.

"Mr. Silver has been asking about you," the doctor said with a smile.

"He has?" Jordan asked, surprised.

"All through the surgery, I'm afraid," the doctor said, not sounding too put out.

"What?" Jordan didn't understand.

"Mr. Silver had a dislocated shoulder we needed to reset and a few cuts that needed suturing," the doctor explained gently. "He was given a local anesthetic to keep him from feeling it, but he was awake the entire time, and very worried about you. If we weren't so swamped here, I would have sent out a nurse to get you. I'm very sorry I kept you waiting this long."

Jordan's smile was reward enough for the doctor, but she actually hugged him too.

"Thank you, thank you, thank you," she chanted.

The doctor laughed softly. "Thank the designer of side and forward airbags, Ms. Tate. They saved Mr. Silver's life."

Jordan nodded, still overjoyed at the news. "Can I see him?"

"Yes, follow me."

The doctor led her to the room where Dylan was sitting up in a bed. He wore his pants but no shirt. He had a bandage on one forearm, a smaller bandage on his upper chest, and one around his ribcage. A shoulder harness kept his left arm in a sling.

Jordan moved to him immediately, and he smiled warmly although it was obvious he was tired.

"Dylan..."

"He's cracked a couple of ribs," the doctor said from behind her. "So be careful when you hug him."

Jordan's gaze shifted to Dylan's eyes. He winked at her, but she could see now that he was breathing gingerly, as if it hurt.

"What happened?" she asked, touching his cheek softly.

Dylan waited until the doctor left before he spoke. "I went to see Marissa, like it said in the note..." His voice trailed off as he breathed heavily. "I thought she wanted to work things out with the divorce, but she talked about having a baby…" He shook his head disbelievingly. His hand took Jordan's and squeezed it gently. "She was crazy, Jordan," he said, his tone changing. "And I'm starting to think she had everything to do with this accident."

"Are you serious?" Jordan asked. "How did the accident happen?"

"A truck tried to run me off the road… That's not what bothers me. What bothers me is what she said right before I left her there. She said she'd kill me before she'd let you have me…"

Jordan drew a sharp breath, her eyes widening as she realized that it probably was indeed Marissa who had tried to kill Dylan on that highway.

Dylan squeezed her hand again. "What I'm worried about," he began, pausing to take a few breaths, "is you. I want you safe, Jordan, you and the baby."

"No, Dylan, we're all going to be safe," Jordan said, her eyes taking on a determined look. "I'll take care of it, don't worry."

Dylan looked back at her for a few moments, then nodded, breathing a sigh of relief. He'd been afraid she'd argue with him on this. She didn't know Marissa. Marissa was vicious enough to do something like this, and Dylan knew that she was behind his accident. And he knew she'd meant for him to end up dead, not just hurt. He also knew that once she knew her plan hadn't worked, she might change tactics. Jordan and the baby might be her next target, and Dylan didn't want Jordan taking any chances.

***

Joe Sinclair was asleep next to his wife. He lay on his stomach, one long arm and a leg thrown over her possessively. When the phone rang, he groaned. His wife stirred, chuckling as she picked up the phone and handed it to him.

"Sinclair." He answered with his last name automatically, having done it for years.

"Joe, it's Jordan," she said, her voice strained.

Joe rubbed his eyes as he turned over on his back, glancing at his wife. "Jordan, how are you?"

"I need your help, Joe," Jordan replied, looking around as the paparazzi pressed closer, hoping to hear her conversation.

Joe sat up, his light blue eyes narrowing. "What's goin' on? What do you need?" he asked, sounding instantly worried.

Jordan took a deep breath, debating whether to tell him on the phone. Finally she sighed. "I can't really explain right now, but can you come?"

"Sure, sure. Where are you?"

"I'm in Los Angeles, at Cedars-Sinai."

"Are you okay?" Joe asked, his worry deepening instantly.

"I'm fine, Joe. I just need you here. I need your protection again."

Joe blew his breath out. "Okay." He glanced at the clock and did a quick calculation. "I can be there inside of three hours. Will that work?"

"That would be great, Joe, thanks," Jordan said, relieved that he was willing to be there for her when she needed him. He'd said he would be, but she hadn't been altogether sure.

They hung up a few moments later.

In San Diego, Joe glanced down to see a pair of teal-colored eyes watching him.

"Jordan needs you?" Randy asked, her tone indecipherable.

Joe nodded, lying down next to her again and putting his hand to her waist to pull her close to him.

"Is it going to bother you, me running off to her aid?" he asked, watching her closely.

Randy looked back at him, her teal eyes unreadable. She was getting good at that. "Should it bother me that you're going to run to her aid?"

Joe narrowed his eyes, a grin tugging at his lips. "Been hanging around Dave too long, haven't you?"

"Now why would you say that?" Randy asked, affecting a totally innocent look.

"Goddamned narcs…" Joe muttered. "Between your brother, your sister-in-law, my cousin, and Dave, I think you're over-saturated."

Randy laughed. Dave Dibbins had been a friend of theirs for years. He was the lead of a narcotics unit that included Randy's brother, Donovan; his wife, Jeanie; and Joe's cousin, Christian; as well as Christian's wife, Stevie.

She sat up and kissed him. His hand slid through her hair, holding her to him as he deepened the kiss. Randy's hand moved to his, sliding down to touch the gold wedding band on his ring finger. He knew what she was thinking. They were married once again, and that gave her all the confidence in him she needed. Joe wasn't the type of man to be unfaithful. He loved his wife. The circumstances that had separated them and caused their divorce had long since been resolved. Things were better with their marriage now than they'd ever been.

Three hours later, Joe strode into Cedars-Sinai. His light blue eyes found Jordan immediately. He saw her mass of dark hair—she was sitting with her back to him, but predictably with a dark-haired man. Joe had known Brenden Sparks would be right there for Jordan; he always was.

"Jordan?"

Jordan stood, and Joe couldn't have been more shocked if his life had depended on it. He saw her belly; although still quite small by normal women's standards, it was obvious she was pregnant.

"Oh my God…" Joe said, breaking into a brilliant smile as he moved to hug her.

"How did this… well, I know how, but when? I mean…" He stumbled over his words, grinning as he realized how it sounded.

Jordan pulled back and looked up at him. She remembered well why she'd loved him. He was handsome, with a strong jawline, long dirty-blond hair, and the most beautiful light blue eyes. He was also the most generous, caring, and masculine man she'd ever known. Until Dylan. Dylan's way was very different from Joe's, but it blended much better with hers.

"I, uh…" She smiled while biting her lip. "I kind of met someone…"

"At least once." Joe winked at her.

Jordan laughed, glad that Joe was obviously not at all uncomfortable with this situation.

"Oh believe me, it was more than once," Brenden put in. "I think they went at it constantly, till they got it just right." He extended his hand to Joe.

Joe took the other man's hand, shaking it and smiling. Joe looked around him. "So why are we here?"

"It's Dylan." Jordan sat down, taking Joe's hand and pulling him to sit next to her. "Dylan Silver. He was in a car accident. A truck tried to run him off the road. He's okay, but he's convinced it was Marissa, his not-soon-enough-to-be ex-wife is behind it. She's crazy, Joe."

"So, she's the one you need protection from?"

"Dylan is convinced she's crazy enough to come after me," Jordan said, nodding. "But I want you to protect Dylan too. I can't take the chance that something could happen to him."

Joe noted how worried she sounded. "Well, I'm all yours," he said. "But I will get some people on investigating that accident. If this woman hired someone to run him off the road, I'll have her put in jail where she belongs."

Jordan breathed a sigh of relief.

Joe made some phone calls, and had people on the case less than a half hour later. His company, Mach 3, a bodyguard business he'd started with John Machiavelli, had contacts in every aspect of law enforcement. Not to mention the fact that he was best friends with the California Attorney General, Midnight Chevalier-Debenshire. Jordan knew that if anyone could stop Marissa Silver, it would be Joe.

****

Dylan lay in the hospital bed, glancing around him and shaking his head. They certainly didn't go for warm and comfortable in these places. He pressed the button on the remote for the TV. Flipping through channels, he settled on VH1; at least there was some music to be found there. He leaned back against the pillows behind his head and closed his eyes.

"Well, you found some music," Jordan said from beside him.

Dylan grinned before even opening his eyes. "Can't keep me here otherwise," he said mildly as he opened his eyes to look at her.

"Figured as much," she said, grinning back at him.

Her eyes trailed over to the door, and Dylan followed her line of sight. He didn't know why he was actually surprised to see Joe Sinclair standing there, but he was. He hid it quite well, his look not changing at all.

"Dylan, this is Joe Sinclair," Jordan said hesitantly.

Dylan nodded. "I've seen his picture," he said, his tone still mild.

Joe looked back at the man Jordan was seeing now and was surprised by his lack of reaction. He'd expected surprise, or at least something to indicate that Joe being there wasn't expected. Maybe Jordan had told him already about calling. Joe couldn't read any emotion at all in the man's eyes, however, and that dragged at him. Why was he hiding? What was he hiding?

Joe took a beat, allowing the silence to stretch just a bit, a habit he'd developed as a cop. A lot of times silence made people nervous and they'd start talking, if for nothing else than to fill the silence. Dylan Silver didn't do anything, merely looking back at Joe calmly.

"Jordan tells me you believe your accident wasn't an accident," Joe said, his voice all cop.

Dylan simply nodded, his eyes not leaving Joe's face.

"You believe the truck that ran you off the road was trying to kill you?" Joe asked, his light blue eyes taking in every aspect of Dylan Silver.

From what Joe could discern, Dylan was tall, with a strong build; since Dylan still wore no shirt, the lean muscle was evident. He was English—Joe had heard that in the accent, which sounded somewhere in the middle class, probably London. Dylan had a strong jawline that showed no sign of tension. Joe also noted silver-gray eyes that seemed quite calm. Dylan Silver was a good-looking guy, but who was he? Joe had never heard of him.

"The truck tried to force me off the road." Dylan's voice didn't show any sort of anger at that thought.

"Off the road?" Joe repeated, shrugging slightly and shaking his head. That didn't necessarily mean the driver of the truck wanted him dead, just out of the way.

"The side I was being forced to has a mile drop-off."

"That would be trying to kill you, then." Joe searched Dylan's face for some sign that the guy was irritated or upset by the idea.

Dylan remained silent, only nodding his head.

"And you think your ex-wife had something to do with it?"

Again Dylan nodded, glancing at Jordan as she narrowed her eyes and grimaced. Dylan took her hand in his and squeezed it.

"What makes you believe that?" Joe asked, taking in the looks exchanged between Dylan and Jordan.

"She told me she'd kill me before she'd let Jordan have me," Dylan replied, very matter of fact.

"When did she say that?" Joe asked.

"Before the accident, I'd gone down to Santa Monica Pier to meet her, to talk, I thought about the divorce. She wanted to talk about getting back together. When I told her that wasn't going to happen, that's when she told me she'd kill me."

Joe looked surprised, but the guy didn't sound too upset about all of this. Was this how he handled stressful situations? Dead calm like this? Joe didn't think he was lying—he obviously had injuries, and most people wouldn't total an $80,000 Jaguar for a scam. Or at least Joe didn't think so; he intended to check it out. Dylan Silver surely didn't have the money that Jordan had, and if the guy was dumping his wife just to marry money, Joe didn't intend to help him. So far, Joe hadn't seen anything in Dylan Silver to indicate what a woman like Jordan was doing with him.

"Can you think of anything else that might help?" Joe asked, his thoughts well hidden behind his light blue eyes.

Dylan thought about it. "She was on her cell phone as I was leaving. I don't know if that means anything."

Joe thought it definitely might mean something. "How far from Santa Monica were you when the accident happened?"

"'Bout a half hour," Dylan said. "Ten minutes from Jordan's place in Malibu."

"I need to make some calls," Joe said, looking at Jordan. "Let me know when you're ready to go back to the house, okay?"

"Okay."

Joe left the room. Dylan leaned back, closing his eyes slowly.

"You okay?" Jordan asked. She'd noticed his manner with Joe; it wasn't like him.

Dylan nodded. "I'm just tired."

"Okay," Jordan said, holding onto his hand. She sat down next to the bed, staying with him for another hour until she noticed he really was dozing off.

"I'll be back tomorrow, okay?" she told him.

Dylan nodded again, his eyes still half closed. He hadn't spoken the entire time she'd been there. Leaning over, she kissed him on the lips. "See you tomorrow," she said softly.

"I'll be here," he said, quirking a grin.

Jordan smiled. "No running off with a cute nurse, okay?"

"I'll try not to." He winked.

Jordan left, feeling better. Maybe he was just tired.

Dylan sat in his hospital room, doing his best to squash the questions in his head. The uppermost of which was why had Jordan called Joe? He rang for the nurse and asked for something to help him sleep, seeking solace in a dreamless medicated slumber.

***

On the drive back to her house, Joe glanced over at Jordan a few times. He was trying to decide whether or not to ask Jordan about Dylan. She wasn't exactly the one to ask whether or not she thought Dylan was lying or had set this up. Maybe he could get around it somehow.

"So, how did you and Dylan meet?" he asked conversationally.

"He helped me write my album," Jordan said, smiling. "He's also now the bassist for my backing band."

"What happened to the other guy?"

"He quit... Well, I fired him, but he quit too." Jordan rolled her eyes. "He got all possessive of me, and when I turned him down he got really confrontational. I finally got sick of it and told him to get the hell out of my studio."

Joe grinned. That was the Jordan he knew. "So Dylan took over?"

"BJ pulled him in. Beege knew I was having problems writing songs, so he brought in Dylan, knowing he could help me."

"Problems writing?" Joe asked, raising an eyebrow at her.

Jordan grimaced. "Well, everything I wrote kind of sounded really... um... pissed off."

"Pissed off?"

"At you," Jordan said, willing to be honest with him now. "At life, at love."

Joe nodded, wincing slightly. "Thought that might be why."

Jordan sighed, putting her forehead against the cool glass of the passenger window of Joe's Escalade. "I didn't want to put out an album that would crucify you, and I didn't want to pretend I wasn't affected by us breaking up." She shrugged. "And I just couldn't come up with anything in between."

"I hear what you did come up with is hitting number one on charts everywhere though."

"You hear?"

Joe rolled his eyes. "So I've kept up with your record a bit, so?"

Jordan chuckled. "Question is, were you brave enough to buy the album?"

"Nope," he said, shaking his head.

"You should." She sat back and looked at him. "We wrote some really incredible songs. I'm even proud of them for a change."

"You mean, you'll actually listen to them voluntarily?" Joe asked, grinning.

"Yes," she said with a laugh.

Joe remembered well what it was like trying to get her to listen to her own stuff when they'd first met. He'd wanted to hear her music, since she wasn't the kind of genre he normally listened to. He'd bought her first two albums in London, and then proceeded to listen to them back to back, having her tell him what had inspired each song. It had been like pulling teeth.

"And Dylan helped you write them?"

Jordan nodded. "He's an incredible writer, Joe. He's won Grammys for his songwriting."

"He has?" Joe asked.

"Have you ever listened to the band Project?" she asked him.

"Yeah, they've been around for years."

"Dylan was the bassist for them," Jordan said. "He also wrote every song they ever did."

"Really?" Joe asked, surprised. He'd already misjudged Dylan Silver.

"Yep," Jordan said, smiling proudly.

Joe canted his head, giving her a sidelong glance. "So what's between you two? The writing, or what?"

Jordan looked at Joe, surprised that he'd come right out and asked, but she realized she shouldn't be. Joe had been very concerned about her when they'd broken up. He'd asked her to call him if she ever felt like she needed him. She'd refused but promised to call Brenden. But Joe worried about her, and Jordan knew that was just how Joe was. He cared about her, so he worried.

Jordan smiled fondly. "Joe, he's an incredible man. You haven't gotten a chance to get to know him yet, but he's just..." She shook her head, unable to put into words how she felt about Dylan. "You have to get to know him to understand, you really do."

Joe nodded, thinking that wasn't really an answer. He wondered if Jordan was just grabbing onto the first man who showed her affection again. He hoped that wasn't the case.

"So, it's safe to assume the baby is his?" Joe asked gently.

"Yes, it's his," she said, smiling. She knew Joe was worried she'd bawl him out for asking. "And just so you know, we're getting married when his divorce is final."

"Really, now?" Joe was surprised by this news, but pleased as well.

At least Dylan Silver was handling his responsibilities. Although, Jordan's money could still be a factor. Joe did guess that Dylan probably had money from being in Project, but a lot of old-time rockers blew through their money as fast as they made it. Joe resolved to look up all he could on Dylan Silver. He wanted to know just what this guy was about.

Later that night, Joe started getting the reports on Marissa Silver. Apparently she was considered the supreme bitch in Hollywood and pretty much everywhere she went. Dylan had always been portrayed as the moneymaker, while Marissa was portrayed as the one who spent his money. She didn't have a job, never had one as best Joe could tell. Dylan Silver was not broke; he was, in fact, quite comfortable, with over four million dollars in the bank and a number of assets to his name. Marissa's name didn't appear anywhere in the Silvers' financial documents. Joe decided Dylan Silver was much smarter than he'd realized originally.

The only place Joe did start seeing Marissa Silver's name was in the tabloids. She was apparently a very indiscreet adulteress. There were reports of her with this guy or that guy, "out on the town," or "leaving the hotel in the wee hours of the morning." The reports went on and on. There were no reports like that on Dylan. The faithful husband? Joe wondered. Obviously he'd slept with Jordan long before his divorce started, so he hadn't always been faithful. But was Jordan the first?

There was also an incident report filed by Cedars-Sinai hospital three years before when Dylan Silver had been treated for a knife wound to his forearm. Marissa was reportedly his attacker. Dylan hadn't pressed charges. So Marissa Silver was violent. It was highly possible that if her golden goose was nesting elsewhere, she was willing to kill him to keep him from divorcing her. Joe wondered mildly if Marissa realized she wasn't Dylan's beneficiary on either his will or his life insurance. She probably didn't; Joe imagined that Dylan had been careful to keep his wife from knowing that part. Joe found that, in fact, Jordan, as well as their unborn child, had been recently added as his beneficiary in both cases. Joe liked the guy more and more, just on principle. He wasn't after Jordan for her money. That was a relief. But Joe still wasn't convinced Jordan wasn't just grabbing the first chance at love again. Joe knew it wasn't really any of his business, but he wanted it settled in his mind.

The following day, while Jordan was in seeing Dylan at the hospital, Joe got a chance to talk to Brenden about Dylan Silver.

With Brenden, Joe could ask straight questions. Brenden was fully aware of Joe's angst over breaking up with Jordan. Brenden would understand that Joe wanted her happy, not clutching at the first guy that came along.

"So what's the deal with this Silver?" Joe asked Brenden as they stood outside in the quad at the hospital, smoking.

Brenden grinned, knowing Joe was being a cop as usual. "In terms of what?"

"In terms of everything," Joe said, then narrowed it down. "Is Jordan the first woman he's cheated on his wife with?"

Brenden gave a short laugh, shaking his head. "No, man, not even close. Dylan's been on the cheat circuit for about ten years now. He's just very low key about it."

"Unlike his wife?"

"Very much so," Brenden said, making a face.

Joe narrowed his eyes. "And you know... from experience?"

Brenden coughed, nodding.

"Is she worth it?" Joe asked, his grin sarcastic.

Brenden shook his head. "Again, not even close."

Joe knew that Brenden had been with countless women over the years. He was the consummate rock-star bad boy, and he'd enjoyed that fame thoroughly.

"He seems awfully... reserved," Joe said, searching for the right word to describe the vibe he got from Dylan Silver.

"Yeah, that's Silver, alright. He's about as cool headed as they come."

Joe gave him a questioning look. "Then what's he doing with someone like Jordan?"

Brenden laughed at that. "I know, I wondered the same thing," he admitted. "But they seem to click pretty well."

Joe looked mystified, shaking his head. "Is he even going to know how to handle her when she goes all dramatic on him?"

"Oh, she has, trust me," Brenden said, grinning. "And he handled her. It's not like he doesn't have experience with the more theatrical side of the feminine gender."

"Oh really?" Joe said, curious in spite of himself.

Brenden laughed and lit another cigarette. "Dylan's dated the cream of the crop of the Hollywood stars and starlets around here. And they have nothing but glowing things to say about the guy. It's disgusting, if you ask me."

"He dates movie stars and no one ever gets wind of it?" Joe asked cynically.

"I told you, he's careful, very low under the radar," Brenden said, gesturing with the flat of his hand to indicate where Dylan kept things.

"None of them ever got pissed that he wouldn't leave his wife?"

"Apparently not," Brenden said, shrugging.

Joe nodded. "He's got to be good, I'll give him that."

Brenden grinned rakishly. "That's what I've heard." His blue-green eyes twinkled mischievously.

"You know someone who slept with him?" This was way beyond Joe's business, but he was curious.

"I know a few women who slept with him."

"And?" Joe asked, leaning back against the wall, waiting.

"And..." Brenden said, "suffice it to say, we're lucky there aren't more men like him out there, or we'd be lookin' like bloody buggers."

Joe gave him a pointed look. "That good?"

Brenden laughed, understanding Joe's thinking. Jordan had proclaimed Joe to be the best lover she'd had, even apologizing to Brenden for putting Joe ahead of him. If Dylan was better, Joe had just been bested. That was never an easy thing for a man to take.

"Relax, man," Brenden said, walking over and clapping Joe on the shoulder. "Your wife loves you, right?"

"Uh-huh." Joe grinned. He knew what Brenden was saying.

The two walked inside, waiting for Jordan to come out. Brenden had come to the hospital to check on Dylan and to make sure Joe had everything he needed to track down information on Marissa Silver.

John Machiavelli arrived at the hospital a few minutes after Brenden left. He gave Joe updates on what he'd found. They'd requested Marissa Silver's cell phone records, and John said they'd have those inside of a day.

"Got a good earful on what a bitch Marissa Silver is this morning too," John said.

"Yeah? From who?"

"Billy Montague." John shook his head.

"How did you see her?" Joe asked, remembering the feisty lead singer of Billy and the Kid.

"She's in the studio with Kid right now, and so's my wife. I ran into her and she asked about you. She's still got a thing for you."

"She has a thing for every man she hasn't slept with, Mackie."

"True." John chuckled. "She also let me know that she'd do anything she could to help Dylan against his wife," he said wryly.

Joe gave him a deadpan look. "Let me guess, she slept with him too?"

John laughed outright at that. "I wouldn't doubt it."

Joe shook his head. None of this jibed with the mild-mannered man he'd met the day before. He was too clean-cut for that. You never did know about the quiet, mild-mannered ones though.

"Okay, well let me know as soon as we get the report on her cell calls. Dylan said she was on the phone when he left her, and that's quite possibly going to be to our truck driver. I don't want to give her too much time to plan something else, you know?"

"Got it," John said, nodding. "I'll call you as soon as I have something."

"Thanks."

John left, and Joe sat down to wait for Jordan to finish her visit. He noticed the paparazzi clicking away on him. He glanced over at them, then turned back to waiting for Jordan. He wasn't fond of having his every move tracked by people and their damned cameras. But he knew it was something he'd have to get used to in this business. It was the reason he didn't do star body-guard work too often. Jordan was an exception to that rule.

In his hospital room, Dylan was getting closer to being his old self. When Jordan walked into the room that morning she noticed he'd put all the earrings back into the holes in his ears. He now sported three small silver hoops, a black stud, and a diamond in the left ear, and two small hoops, a black stud, and a diamond stud in the right ear. It was how she was used to seeing him. It showed his wild side.

Her fingers brushed the earrings as she kissed him.

"I see you talked some poor nurse out of your belongings."

"I told her I was naked without these," he said, flicking his fingers toward the earrings.

Jordan smiled. "What else did you talk her out of, Dylan Silver?" she asked, narrowing her eyes.

He looked back at her in an attempt to look innocent, his impertinent grin spoiling the effect.

"Uh-huh…" she said, giving him a dirty look.

Dylan touched her under the chin, pulling her to him, and kissed her softly.

"I love you."

"Okay, you're forgiven."

"Works every time."

Jordan gasped, then laughed. She was glad he was back to normal now. They'd told him he could leave the hospital that evening.

131

When she left that morning, she promised to be back in plenty of time to pick him up and take him back to her house where he belonged. Dylan nodded, already getting tired again.

Later that afternoon, Jordan and Joe arrived back at the hospital to a scene. Jordan was stunned to see Marissa Silver standing in Dylan's hospital room. When Marissa saw Jordan, her eyes narrowed. Dylan was sitting on the bed, his look as calm as ever. Jordan saw red immediately and started toward Marissa. Joe grabbed her before she got a foot away from him. Dylan grinned mildly.

"What the fuck are you doing here?" Jordan asked angrily, struggling against Joe's hold to no avail.

"Visiting my husband," Marissa replied, her tone cutting.

"Get out!"

"I don't think so," Marissa said condescendingly.

"I think so," Dylan said, unagitated.

Marissa shot him a dirty look. "My husband was in a car accident," she began, puffing herself up with importance.

"Two nights ago," Dylan put in.

Marissa whirled on him. "It's not my fault the fucking police don't bother calling the wife of the victim anymore!"

Dylan nodded, looking totally composed.

"Don't give me that smug fucking look, Dylan. I won't put up with that shit from you!" Marissa yelled, balling up her fist.

Dylan merely raised an eyebrow at her.

"I think it's time you leave," Joe said, his voice low, the threat in it evident.

"I think you should stay the hell out of this!" Marissa screamed at him.

Joe put Jordan behind him and took a step toward Marissa.

"Joe." Dylan shook his head slightly, holding up a finger for Joe to wait a minute. "Marissa," he said calmly, "you need to leave now."

"Don't tell me what to do, Dylan!" Her face was suffused with angry color.

"Either I tell you, or he tells you," Dylan said, nodding at Joe. "And I'm thinking that his way might be a bit more embarrassing for you."

Marissa looked at Joe, taking in the broad shoulders and the fighter's stance.

"What is it you think you can do?" Marissa asked Joe, never willing to back down automatically.

Joe gave her a wintery smile. "I can frog-march your ass out of here by a handful of hair and clothing, or I can do it in cuffs," he said, pulling a pair out of his back pocket and holding them up by one finger.

"You wouldn't dare!"

"Bet me," Joe replied, the ice in his light blue eyes matching his tone.

Marissa glanced at Dylan; he merely looked back at her serenely. She gave him a vile look, then strode toward the door. Joe moved back to allow her out, keeping an arm out to block Jordan from attacking at the same time.

As soon as Marissa was gone, Jordan turned to Dylan.

"What the hell was she doing here?"

Dylan shrugged. "She just walked in."

"Why didn't you make her leave?"

Dylan paused, mild amusement in his eyes. "I'm not up to manhandling my ex-wife out of a hospital room at this point," he said, his tone completely calm.

Jordan stared back at him, then blew her breath out. She walked over and touched his cheek.

"I'm sorry," she said. "I guess I was still reacting to her, wasn't I?"

Dylan smiled. "Just a bit."

Jordan lowered her head, looking up at him. "I'm sorry."

Dylan didn't reply; he merely put his hand to her cheek, pulling her toward him and kissing her lips softly.

Joe watched with interest. Dylan Silver definitely knew how to handle Jordan's drama—he just sat back and waited for her to blow herself out. Of course this was a mild one. All the same, Joe had to hand it to Dylan. He was far from what Jordan was used to with her men. Maybe that's what made the difference.

That evening, Joe had a few other surprises. For one thing, in escorting Dylan out of the hospital, he noticed the earrings that hadn't been present the first time he'd met him. The earrings took away from the clean-cut look Dylan had had at first glance. They gave him a bit of an edge that Joe wouldn't have credited him with before.

The second surprise came that night when, after a short rest, Dylan walked into the kitchen wearing only white cotton drawstring pants. As Dylan leaned down to kiss Jordan, Joe got a look at his back. He saw the huge panther tattoo across his shoulders. It was the last thing he'd expected to see. Dylan didn't look like the tattoo type... yet there it was, plain as day, and not some tiny little thing, but a panther that spanned his upper back. Its paws draped over each shoulder, its face in between his shoulder blades. Joe could only imagine how much work it had taken.

Joe's surprise was reflected on his face when Dylan moved back and walked to the refrigerator to get himself a drink.

"What?" Jordan asked.

"Nothing," he said, his eyes on Dylan's back again.

Dylan poured himself some orange juice and sat on the chair next to Jordan.

"Are you hurting at all?" Jordan asked Dylan.

Dylan shook his head. "Took a Vicodin before I went to sleep, remember?"

"Oh yeah," she said, grinning.

"Trying to kill me already?" Dylan asked, a grin of his own on his lips.

"Yeah, that's my plan," she replied, winking at him.

Dylan didn't reply, sitting back in his chair and pulling one knee up to his chest. Jordan grimaced. She closed her eyes for a moment, then opened one and looked at Dylan.

"Your daughter is practicing again."

Dylan leaned forward and put his hand on her stomach. "Come on, Devin..."

As if on cue, Dylan's hand jumped slightly. Dylan smiled brilliantly, glancing at Joe.

"She's going to be a world-class soccer player," he told Joe.

Joe smiled. "You already know it's a girl?"

Dylan looked at Jordan, who rolled her eyes guiltily. "You know me, I like to know what the future holds."

Joe nodded. "And her name is going to be Devon?"

"Devin with an I," Jordan said. "Devin Skye."

"Silver," Dylan added.

"Silver," Jordan repeated with a smile.

Joe noticed the happiness in Jordan's eyes when she said the last name. She really was in love with this guy. And Dylan was becoming more and more likable.

***

A couple of days after he got home from the hospital, Dylan was sitting on Jordan's deck, smoking. Jordan walked out onto the deck and turned to stare at him, her hands on her hips.

"Are you nuts?" she asked him without preamble.

Joe stood near the pool, keeping an eye on things while Dylan was out in the open, so he witnessed the entire conversation. Dylan looked up at her, perplexed.

"Not that I know of, why?" he answered, his tone as even as always.

"You're just handing Marissa the townhouse in London?" she asked sharply.

Dylan didn't answer. He looked back at her, waiting for the rest.

"Sharkey called," Jordan said, holding up his cell phone. "I told him you were trying to rest. He said he was confirming that you wanted to let Marissa have the townhouse in London free and clear. And again, I ask, are you fucking crazy?"

Dylan sat back, lighting another cigarette and taking a long draw. Finally he shrugged. "What do I need a townhouse in London for? I live in the States now. It's just real estate."

"It's the principle of the thing, Dylan. Jesus! You said it was worth two million, You're just going to hand her all this shit she never earned?"

Dylan looked considering, then shrugged. "The townhouse in London, yes."

Jordan stared at him open mouthed, then shook her head, giving him a disgusted look. "She's going to take everything, Dylan, isn't she? You're just going to let her, rather than fight her. Why?"

Again Dylan merely looked back at her, his face impassive. "I know what I'm doing, Jordan," he told her, calm even in the face of her anger.

"Sure you do," Jordan said, sounding like she believed anything but that. "Fine, whatever." She tossed his cell phone at him and strode into the house.

Dylan watched her go, then leaned back against his lounge chair. He closed his eyes and continued to smoke. Joe watched. He'd expected Dylan to at least explain what he was doing, or go after Jordan when she stormed off. He'd done neither. Joe knew he'd have done at least one of those, if not get into a big fight with her over who had the right to do what with their own money and property.

Dylan made no move to go into the house. In fact, he sat on the deck and smoked two more cigarettes, and it didn't even look like he was the least bit agitated. Joe knew what it was like living with and fighting with Jordan; that was part of what had broken them up.

When Dylan went into the house a while later, Joe followed. Dylan proceeded to go into the living room, sit at Jordan's piano, and start writing. Joe wandered around the house, ascertaining where Jordan was. He knew she wouldn't have left the house without him, but he liked to know where she was at all times. She was lying on her bed, her eyes closed.

It was just getting dark when Dylan went into Jordan's bedroom. Joe walked by just then to check on her again. Glancing into the room, he saw Dylan lie down on the bed next to Jordan. She reached out and touched his chest. Joe couldn't help but watch, curious in spite of himself to hear what would happen.

"I'm sorry," Jordan said softly. "I know it's none of my business what you do in your divorce. It's your money and your property."

"You just need to trust me, babe."

"I know. I'm sorry I got mad at you," she said, moving closer to him on the bed.

He slid his hand through her hair, pulling her to him. His lips kissed hers, deepening the kiss a moment later as he held her to him. Jordan moaned softly.

Joe closed the bedroom door quietly, once again amazed by Dylan Silver. The man handled Jordan like a pro. It was like a magic spell he cast over her.

Joe went back to check on them an hour later. Hearing moans and sighs through the door, he walked away grinning. He spent the next six hours attempting to do a final check on them for the night. It was finally silent around two o'clock the next morning. He waited a full minute longer, not wanting to invade their privacy, but knowing he needed to check to make sure they were indeed okay. He didn't want to wake them, so he opened the door quietly and noted they were both still. Walking inside, he checked the windows; one was open, so he closed it gently, looking outside.

"Joe?" Jordan said quietly.

He turned to look down at her. She lay in front of Dylan. His arms were around her from behind, his body wrapped around hers, his head just above hers on the pillow, his lips against her head. He was asleep.

"Sorry, did I wake you?" Joe asked softly.

"It's okay. Is everything alright?"

"Yeah," Joe said. "I've been trying to do my final check on you two for about six hours now."

Jordan laughed softly. "Sorry," she said, her smile brilliant.

"Sure you are," he said, grinning at her.

Jordan bit her lip, her eyes shining in the darkened room.

"Get some sleep," he said. "I'll see you two in the morning."

"Okay." She snuggled back against Dylan happily.

Joe walked to the door of the bedroom, glancing back at Jordan and Dylan again. Brenden had been right about Dylan Silver's prowess; that was certainly true. Joe smiled to himself as he closed the door. It was good to see Jordan so happy.

The morning after their argument, and six-hour make-up session, Dylan and Jordan slept in. When they did get up, Jordan put on her bathrobe after brushing out her hair. Dylan found in trying to get out of bed that he was extremely sore from the exertions to his injured ribs. Jordan felt instantly guilty.

"Why should you feel bad?" he asked, grinning. "I certainly wasn't complaining, or hesitating."

"Yes, but you just got out of the hospital I should practice more self-control."

Dylan placed his hand under her chin, his fingers caressing her cheek. "Uh-uh." He kissed her softly. "Self-control isn't allowed in our bed."

Jordan smiled at him. "Well, I could practice it better when I open my mouth about things that aren't my business."

Dylan grew serious.

"Jordan," he began softly, "it is your business, what I'm doing with my assets. You're the woman I'm planning to marry when my divorce is final. What I bring to this marriage is your business. I just want you to understand that I do know what I'm doing in this."

Jordan winced, nodding her head. "I'm sorry, I know..."

"Actually," he said, settling on his back and pulling her against him, "you really don't, do you?"

Jordan looked at him quizzically.

"You don't know that I know what I'm doing," he explained. "You probably have no idea that I've always kept very close tabs on every penny I make, and every penny she spent. I also keep very careful records of what my assets are." He pinned her with a look. "Four million."

"You're worth four million?" She was surprised by the amount, but she wasn't sure why.

Dylan grinned, shaking his head. "That's what I have in the bank," he said. "Not counting a fair-sized portfolio of stocks and properties."

Jordan stared at him. But then she shook her head. "I wouldn't care if you had nothing, Dylan. That wasn't why I was mad. I just don't like her grabbing everything she can, when she never did anything to make any of it."

"I know," he said. "But I want you to understand that I'm not handing her everything. I'm giving her what I want to give her, things that I don't feel I need to take into this marriage with you. I want you to know what you're getting."

"I know what I'm getting," Jordan said. "I'm getting a man who understands me in ways no one ever has before. A man who loves me regardless of all my faults. A man who won't walk away, even when I'm being the biggest bitch on Earth. That's what I'm getting, Dylan. The money doesn't matter."

Dylan smiled softly. "Well, it does matter to me, in that I want to bring to this marriage something to show for my time in the business. Besides, I fully intend to take good care of my new wife and daughter. And if that means a new car every month, or three townhouses in London, then that's what it will be."

Jordan understood what he was saying. She understood that he had to feel like he wasn't coming into this marriage empty handed, and he certainly wasn't. She kissed him deeply.

"Just so you know," she said, "I would have married you if you didn't have a penny to your name."

"Just so you know," he repeated, "I wouldn't have come to you until I had something to bring."

Jordan narrowed her eyes at him, and he narrowed his right back. She grinned; so did he.

"Another thing you need to know," he said, looking serious again. "If anything should happen to me—"

"Dylan, don't say that," she said sharply, looking alarmed. "Nothing is going to happen to you."

"I know, but if something did," he said, putting his fingers over her lips. "I need you to know that I've changed both my will and my life insurance to name you and the baby as my beneficiaries."

Jordan looked at him, her gold eyes wide, then she shook her head. "Nothing is going to happen to you," she repeated resolutely.

Dylan nodded. He knew she didn't want to think that way. But Dylan always considered eventualities—it was the realistic side of his nature. He just wanted her to know that she was covered.

"When did you do that?" she asked after a few minutes.

Dylan smiled. "Well, I changed it first the day I got back from Vegas and filed for a divorce."

"First?"

"To name you."

She stared at him for a moment. "But you didn't even know why I'd taken off, did you?"

"No," he said, shaking his head. "But I knew you were what I wanted, and I intended to get you back. I figured I needed to take care of my end of it first, however."

"Did it occur to you at all that I might not want you?" she asked with a speculative look.

Dylan shrugged. "No," he said. "You needed me, I could feel it. I knew I just had to get it through your stubborn head."

Jordan smiled at him. "So you knew back in Vegas?"

"Babe, I knew the first time I made love to you," he said softly.

Jordan bit her lip, feeling tears sting her eyes. "I didn't want to believe I could love anyone again," she said, her voice full of emotion. "But you..." She touched his cheek. "You were too good to be true."

"As were you, my love," he replied, leaning down to kiss her lips again.

"Uh-huh." She laughed. "Attitude and all, right?"

"If you didn't have an attitude, Jordan, you wouldn't be you," he said. "I love everything about you, including your attitude."

Jordan sighed, snuggling her head against his neck. "I never thought I could feel this good again."

"I never thought I'd discover love."

She looked up, her eyes searching his. "Just like that?"

"Just like that."

She smiled, snuggling close to him again. Just then the baby kicked; Dylan felt it against his stomach.

"Oh really now?" he asked, reaching down to touch her belly.

Jordan lay on her back, and Dylan pushed the sides of her bathrobe aside to put his face against her stomach.

"Now, listen, Devin. You need to understand that your mommy is going to be number one for a while. You'll get to be number one when you get out here," he said, grinning when he felt the baby move.

"She's moving toward your voice." Jordan smiled as she put her hand into his hair, caressing his head.

"That's because she knows who's buying her her first car, don't you, baby girl?"

Jordan felt movement in her belly, and then it felt like her skin was being stretched right where Dylan's lips touched her stomach. She looked down.

"Oh my God, Dylan, I'd swear that was a hand." She ran her fingers over the spot where it did indeed look like the points of fingers were pressing against Jordan's skin. "I think she's trying to touch you, Daddy," Jordan told him, smiling with tears in her eyes.

Dylan kissed the little points. "You'll just have to wait, little one," he said. "But God already knows I'll probably be wrapped around every little digit you have."

Jordan laughed softly, glancing up and noticing Joe standing in the doorway. His smile was warm. Their eyes connected, and Jordan sensed Joe's complete approval of Dylan as the man in her life.

Indeed, Joe was feeling infinitely better about Dylan Silver. Especially seeing and hearing that his daughter, while still in the womb, so obviously loved her father. Jordan's love for him shone in her eyes as he talked to his unborn child. It was such a complete contrast— this man, with his earrings and his tattoo, but with such a soft voice as to have a child reaching out to touch him before she ever even met him... it said a lot. It said it all. Joe was extremely happy that he'd witnessed it.

Three days later, Joe felt they had enough information on the truck that had run Dylan off the road to execute a search warrant. Contacting John Machiavelli's connection with the sheriff's office, Joe got a warrant written up and went in with the team. They found a description of Dylan's car and his plate number, as well as a map that outlined the direction Dylan would take from the Santa Monica Pier to Jordan's Malibu home. The area where Dylan's crash had occurred was circled in red. Joe used the information to confront the driver of the truck. The driver gave Marissa Silver up immediately, saying that she'd failed to pay him the other half of his money.

Joe got an arrest warrant issued for Marissa Silver, but she couldn't be located. Joe set people on her trail, and stuck with Dylan and Jordan.

***

A week after Dylan's accident, Brenden contacted Dylan about working on a greatest hits album for Project. It was something they'd talked about when Dylan had opted out of their contract with Badlands. Brenden hadn't given up the idea that Project might get back together, although Brenden doubted that Dylan would continue to be the bassist for the band if they did. Brenden knew that Dylan would stay with Jordan's band, since being in her band meant he and Jordan would be together all the time. Jordan needed that. Someone to be with her all the time. That's why things had been difficult with Joe. Joe had refused to give up his life to be with Jordan. Jordan had resented that, no matter how much she understood that Joe had had a life before she'd met him.

Dylan said he'd be more than happy to work on some re-mixes of Project songs. Brenden also brought up the idea that maybe Dylan could write a few new songs for the album, since he had apparently gotten over his block now. Dylan agreed it would be a good idea.

Within two weeks, Dylan was traveling to the studio to work on rewrites for some of Project's previous hits. They were revamping and updating songs. Songs that had been hits on the first few albums needed a new polish. Dylan had an ear for perfection when it came to music, so he was the one to sit with the sound man to work on the new versions. The band was in the studio. Van Strat, the lead singer, was at the mic. Joe was sitting in the sound booth watching the process with interest.

"Van," Dylan said, depressing the intercom button for the studio, "that was a little flat. Can you try it again?"

Van shook his mane of blond hair. "It wasn't flat, D. You're hearing things."

"Van, just do it again, man," said the lead guitarist, Jack Bennings.

"It wasn't flat," Van said, his voice tightly controlled.

Joe glanced at Dylan, who was nodding to himself, hitting a series of buttons.

"Just cue it up, Dylan, and stop fucking around," Van said derisively.

Dylan nodded again, totally unperturbed. He continued doing exactly as he had been, ignoring Van's irritated looks and annoyed sighs.

Jack just shook his head knowingly.

The next minute the playback flowed through the speakers of both the sound booth and the studio. It played for thirty seconds, then cut off.

"First take," Dylan said calmly.

A second bar of music flowed through the speakers, and everyone heard it at the same time. Van's voice dropped a note right in the middle of a section. Van even grimaced when he heard it.

"Second," Dylan said unnecessarily.

Joe glanced at Dylan once again. To his surprise, there was absolutely no gloating in his look or attitude. He simply sat watching Van through the windows.

"You were right," Van said, making a face.

"You should no better than to counter him, Van," Jack said, shaking his head and grinning.

Van gave him a vile look. "Fuck you, Jack."

"Not till you've had a shower."

"And a sex change," added the drummer, Billy Kaine.

Dylan grinned in the sound booth, then cued up the music again.

Joe was fascinated watching Dylan work in the studio. His fingers flew across the sound board, making adjustments and calling for retakes. When he felt something needed to be stronger or held longer he'd ask for it to be redone. Most of the time the members of Project didn't argue with him. They knew Dylan had a producer's ear. He could hear when something wasn't right. What many people didn't know, even fewer people than knew Dylan had written every one of their songs, was that Dylan also was chief on sound and producing the album. He had an intrinsic ability to hear what was right and what wasn't. It was a gift. He could always produce albums if he never worked as a musician again.

It quickly became clear to Joe that Dylan was the very backbone of the band. He ran it, whether he was the lead singer, the front man, or not.

On the way back to Jordan's that evening, Joe looked over at Dylan. He'd seen the other members of Project get irritable and snap, but not Dylan. He always maintained an even tone, even when he'd been snapped at.

"Are you always this calm?" Joe asked.

Dylan grinned, glancing over at Joe. Then he shrugged. "I guess I am."

Joe shook his head in amazement. "How do you do it? I would have snapped a few times today."

Dylan thought about it for a moment, then shrugged again. "I've never been much on temper. I grew up in a household that was very stable. My parents never raised their voices, either to me or to each other. I guess I grew up thinking that was the civil way to handle things."

"Well, it is, ideally," Joe agreed. "But I could never manage it."

"Don't you have to as a police officer?" Dylan asked curiously.

"Yeah, but that's on the job."

Dylan hooked his thumb back toward the studio. "That's my job."

Joe chuckled. "Yeah, but rock stars are known to be temperamental."

Dylan laughed, agreeing with that. "But bassists are known to be the grounded ones in the group. We're the steady backbeat. Not flashy, not flamboyant, but always there."

Joe glanced over at him again, his look quizzical. "And that's the personality you have. Stable, sensible, responsible, steady."

"And in the background," Dylan added.

"And that's what works so well with Jordan," Joe said, making a realization as he said it. "You don't steal her spotlight, nor do you care to."

Dylan looked back at Joe, his face telling Joe that he already knew that.

"And that was the problem with me and Jordan," Joe said, grimacing. "My life stole her spotlight constantly. The nature of what I do, my family, my friends, even me."

"Can't have two dynamic personalities in the same relationship without a lot of fire."

Joe nodded. "I know. My two best friends are like that. Rick and Midnight are a consistent love–hate relationship."

"Midnight?" Dylan queried. "Would that be the State Attorney General, Midnight?"

"That would be the one," Joe said with a smile.

"Very intriguing woman."

"Indeed."

"You've known her a long time?" Dylan asked, curious in spite of himself.

"'Bout twenty-two years now."

"And she's always been so... engaging?"

"Very," Joe said.

Dylan grinned.

***

The following day, Jordan opted to accompany Joe and Dylan to the studio. Dylan himself was in the studio this time, working on basslines for the rewrites. Jordan sat in the studio with him. Joe sat in the sound booth, watching. They were two hours into the session when Marissa Silver burst into the studio. Joe was up and out of his chair a second later and heading into the studio from the sound booth. Unfortunately, the sound engineer needed to buzz him in, and the guy was fixated on what was happening in the studio.

Marissa walked in, her eyes on Jordan immediately, who was sitting at the far side of the room.. Jordan looked back at Marissa, sensing the tension in the other woman. She moved to stand, and everything happened at once. Dylan stepped closer to Jordan. Marissa brought her arm up. There was a flash of metal, and Jordan saw Dylan's arm slash through the air. Jordan didn't see the knife Marissa had just thrown at her, not until it clattered to the floor, knocked there by Dylan's quick movement. Marissa screamed, seeing her attack thwarted, and launched herself at Dylan.

Inside the sound booth, Joe yelled at the sound engineer to buzz him in. The man came out of his trance and hit the button, and Joe was through the door a moment later. He moved directly to Marissa Silver, grabbing her arm that was clawing at Dylan. With his other arm, Joe pushed Jordan back—she was trying to help Dylan. Joe didn't know if Marissa had another weapon, and he wasn't taking any chances. Bringing Marissa's arm up behind her back, he took her to the floor, and Dylan stepped back.

"Let go of me, sonofabitch!" Marissa screeched.

Joe glanced up at the sound engineer. "Call the cops," he said. "Mrs. Silver has a date with a booking sergeant."

"You can't arrest me! Do you know who I am?"

Joe grinned to himself as he hauled her up off the floor, having cuffed her.

"You're the psychotic nut that's going to jail?" Joe said politely.

"Let go of me!" Marissa started to struggle.

Joe lifted her arms a little higher, making her cry out. "Don't make me break your arms."

Marissa quieted instantly.

"Dylan, you're bleeding!" Jordan exclaimed, moving to his side and touching his forearm.

Dylan looked at his arm, made a face, and then shrugged. "It doesn't hurt."

Joe leaned over and looked at Dylan's arm. "You'll need stitches."

"I want her out of my studio," Brenden said from the doorway.

He'd heard that Marissa Silver had been spotted entering the building, and he had headed down to the studio Dylan was in just in case. He'd been told by the sound engineer what had happened.

"The police are here," the sound engineer said, passing the word on from security at the front.

Joe nodded and walked Marissa toward the doors. Marissa turned to Dylan, her expression pleading.

"Don't let them do this to me, Dylan. You love me still, I know you do!" she cried.

Dylan looked back at her for a long moment. "I couldn't afford you anymore."

Marissa narrowed her eyes at him, and Joe felt her tense.

"Don't even think about it," Joe said, his tone low and threatening. "Or I'll let him give you the beating you sound like you've needed for a long time."

With that Joe walked her out of the studio.

Brenden looked at Dylan. "You need to get that looked at."

"I know," Dylan said, nodding.

"I'll take him," Jordan said.

An hour and a half later, Dylan had his arm stitched. The cut looked worse than it was; it took only five stitches. Joe had Marissa booked into the L.A. County jail, and filed the appropriate paperwork. He met Dylan and Jordan back at her house. Jordan thanked him for all his help, hugging him gratefully. Dylan shook Joe's hand, also thanking him.

Jordan walked Joe out to his Escalade and hugged him again.

"I'm very happy for you," Joe said.

Jordan bit her lip, smiling at him. "You like him?"

"Very much," he said, putting his finger to Jordan's lips. "At first I wasn't sure if he was right for you, but I can see he is much more right for you than I ever was."

"I never would have believed it, Joe," she said, understanding what Joe was saying. "I would never have pictured myself with someone like Dylan. He's so mild mannered, so quiet, but I really think that's what I need."

"I think you're right. And I'm glad I got a chance to see you two together, and you so happy."

"I think that's why I called you," she said. "Because I knew you needed absolution from the guilt I knew you were feeling about us."

Joe nodded. "You have no idea."

"Oh, I think I do, Joe," Jordan replied. "I know you, remember? You feel bad if you can't fix everyone."

"Well, you fixed yourself, didn't you?"

"I think Dylan did a lot of fixing too," she said, smiling fondly.

"Maybe," Joe said. "But you're strong, and you know what you want. You stuck to that, and in the end you'll have it all."

Jordan narrowed her eyes. "I think you gave me no choice about sticking to it. If you hadn't broken up with me, I probably would have given up on having children and even getting married."

"That's what I was most afraid of for you, Jordan," he said seriously.

"I know. I'd fooled myself into thinking it was enough for me to have you. But you were right. I really did want kids. I'd forgotten how much until I got pregnant, then I knew I wanted the baby, even when I didn't believe I'd ever have Dylan."

"Well, I'm glad you got both." He leaned down to kiss her on the cheek.

Jordan wrapped her arms around his neck, hugging him again. "Me too," she said, smiling.

♪ Epilogue ♪

Jordan had their daughter, Devin Skye Silver, one day after her due date. Dylan was by her side, coaching her all the way. He was even allowed to cut the cord. When they handed Jordan her daughter, she was wailing up a storm. Jordan reached her finger out, touching Devin's hand. Devin wrapped her tiny fingers around her mother's, and Jordan's smile couldn't have been brighter. Dylan watched his soon-to-be wife and daughter with a warm smile, then leaned down to kiss Jordan softly on the lips and then kiss Devin on the head.

It was another six months before Dylan's divorce was final. Marissa received the townhouse in London, a lump sum of two million dollars, and $25,000 a month alimony; they split the portfolio of stocks. Marissa asked for the house in Bel Air, and Dylan agreed to give it to her for two million dollars. Marissa argued, but finally gave in and had to return the two million he'd given her. In the end, she sold the London townhouse to pay for her lawyers, assuming she'd sue Dylan, Jordan, and Joe Sinclair for millions for slander and win.

Jordan Tate and Dylan Silver were married in a private ceremony, shared with only a few close friends. Brenden, Allexxiss, and Tabitha and her husband, Devlin McGregor, were there. Joe and Randy were there as well. The members of Jordan's band were also present. Jordan's father even flew in from England to attend and see his new granddaughter. Her father walked Jordan down the aisle and gave her to Dylan.

Jordan wore a very pretty dress of antique brocade and lace. It was off the shoulder and tea length. She looked exquisite with her hair flowing around her face. Dylan looked handsome in black tails. They had no attendants, but Dylan held their daughter, who was dressed in a tiny brocade and lace dress. During the ceremony Devin was oddly quiet. When the priest asked if anyone had any reason these two should not be wed, Devin made a small cry.

"Quiet, you," Dylan said with a smile.

Everyone laughed, including the priest. Jordan looked at her daughter, smiling happily.

"I see what you mean," Randy told Joe in a whisper. "She looks so happy."

Joe nodded and smiled.

"You're relieved, aren't you?" she asked, not for the first time.

"Yes."

"Me too," Randy said with a grin.

Joe chuckled softly.

The reception was held at a local Malibu restaurant. They had a room to themselves. There was a small wedding cake, and Brenden toasted the couple.

"I never thought there'd be a man good enough to marry my best friend," Brenden said, his eyes on Jordan. "But she managed to not only find him but snag him away from his wife." He winked at Jordan.

"It wasn't easy," Jordan said, grinning.

"Took your ex-boyfriend to help you," Brenden agreed. "Lucky for us, he was still speaking to you." He raised his glass. "Here's to Dylan and Jordan. May you two always be as happy as you are now, and may Dylan never run out of his seemingly endless supply of patience."

"I'm about to run out of mine," Jordan said, giving Brenden a narrowed look, garnering a laugh from the rest of the group.

Brenden gave Dylan a wink. "It'll happen a lot," he told Dylan in a stage whisper.

"Beege..." Jordan warned.

Brenden laughed. "To life, love, and all that comes with it," he said, raising his glass again.

They had their first dance to the song they'd written together, "Calm the Storm." The song said everything that they were about. Dylan was the calm to Jordan's storm. As they danced, everyone looked on, seeing how much love passed between them. Dylan took Devin from Allexxiss and held his daughter, his arm around Jordan as well. Everyone could see how proud Dylan was to be a father, and Jordan seemed to have mellowed after giving birth to her daughter.

The trial of Marissa Silver took place a week later. Dylan refused to allow Jordan to even attend. He went in long enough to testify. He told the jury about the previous attacks on him by his wife, and about her statement that she'd kill him before she let Jordan have him. Marissa was convicted the following day of aggravated assault with a deadly weapon, and solicitation of murder. She was sentenced to ten to twenty-five years in prison. She claimed her innocence the entire trial, attempting to blame Jordan for framing her. No one would listen.

The album Dylan and Jordan had written together hit number one and stayed there for a record number of weeks. They were nominated for numerous Grammy awards, and Jordan even received a nomination for her songwriting. It was a happy time. Love had come to them like quicksilver, and now they were holding on to it with both hands.

You can find more information about the author and series here:
www.sherrylhancock.com
www.facebook.com/SherrylDHancock

Also by Sherryl D. Hancock:

The *WeHo* **series** follows a group of women from Los Angeles as they navigate the ups and downs of love, life, work, and everything in between.
www.vulpine-press.com/we-ho

The *MidKnight Blue* **series** takes us on a journey with Midnight Chevalier, the tough ex-gang leader who switches sides and works to put away those she used to fight beside.
www.vulpine-press/midknight-blue-series